Canned

Written by Lisa Sa

Illustrated by Giorgi Paikidze

© 2017 Lisa Sa

All rights reserved. No part of this publication may be reproduced, stored in a retrieval system, or transmitted, in any form or by any means, electronic, mechanical, photocopying, recording or otherwise, except as permitted by the UK Copyright, Designs and Patents Act 1988, without the prior permission of the publisher.

ISBN 978-0-244-61070-8

To everyone in my life that loves me exactly the way I am.

Canned Tuna

The Three Month Deadline

It had been three months since they had decided to cut ties. Three months since they had destroyed each other. And she had recently started writing about it, letting the pain resurface in order to put the memories on paper. Writing about him was therapeutic; soothing to the soul. After the perpetuating fear of cutting ties, it was finally done. It was scary as hell, I mean there's nothing us humans dread more than the thought of something we love never returning, permanently gone from our existence. But with time we adapt. Even if we are never quite the same person again.

The girl knew it would be for the best, that the suffering would be worth it in the long term. Or at least, that's what she told herself.

"We are better off apart," she told her friend one evening, who nodded in agreement. The very next day however, as the girl left the office for lunch with a smile, she got out her phone to find a familiar number on her screen.

What do you do when that ex you've started writing about, that ex that has no idea you still think about him every day, that you are still in love with him, sends you a text three months after you have cut ties?

She found the text intrusive, as if he were bursting back into her life uninvited. She wanted to push him out again and tear up his imaginary invitation.

"You are not welcome here!" She would scream in a huff.

The girl stared at the message for hours, repeating the lines in her head obsessively, going over all the possible questions he could want to ask.

What could he possibly want? She asked herself.

Maybe he needs me as a writer on a project. Or he hurt his back again. But the girl knew deep down it would turn out to be none of those reasons, that the only purpose of texting her was to get her back in his life. To reconnect.

And we all know what happens when we reconnect, she thought to herself.

Their cycle was unhealthy and cruel, yet they were drawn to it like moths to a flame.

Not this time.

I will continue to write about him, about everything that happened, for as long as I need to, but I will never go back.

I can't ever go back.

How it Began

The First Date

"Do you believe in love?" asked the cold, arrogant man wearing a Dolce & Gabbana shirt and way too much gel in his hair. He sat opposite me, whiskey in hand, and a curious smile on his face. He was a good-looking man; olive skin, chiseled jaw, and big brown, bastard-eyes. That's what I called them. I had come up with the name three seconds into meeting him, based purely on the fact that I could tell he was a bastard, that he deceived women on a day-to-day basis. And above all else, that he was not to be messed with. The problem was, I saw all of this as an alluring challenge. He needed to be squashed, his ego shattered, and I was going to be the person to do it.

I bit my lip to stop myself from laughing, as I repeated his question in my head.

Do I believe in love?!

His game strategy is poor, I thought. *Who the hell asks that question on a first date?*

Someone who wants to score, that's who.

In the two hours we had been sat at that table in the corner of some dingy bar in Maiden Vale, he had already told me five times that he liked being alone, that he would never change. I knew his game plan and his tactics, so why was I still sitting there? Why hadn't I just walked out?

I had been able to see right through him from the exact moment I had met him. I knew his next move before he did, yet it was effortlessly entertaining to watch it unfold. I sat there in my sexy dress and cocky smile, pretending I had no idea of the façade he was putting on to win. But little did he know that I was going to win that night, by walking out at the end of the evening and never seeing him again.

It didn't mean I couldn't be amused until then though; I was enjoying this game way too much. I was enjoying pretending I was exactly who he saw me to be. Humans are funny like that – stay in the box they put you in and they will forever remain loyal to their perception of you.

"I do. But not for me, just for other people." *Whoops. Too much wine there.*

Bastard-eyes gave me a confused look. "You believe in love for other people? Why not for yourself?" he asked, pretending he cared about my answer, when I knew he was instead wondering what it would be like to rip off my dress.

"No one seems to be interesting enough," I explained to him, "I'm slightly fussy. Love is a big word."

"Indeed it is. We're friends, right? So let me ask you this: You're really looking forward to winning, aren't you?"

I froze. *Hang on, what?* "What do you mean?" I managed to say.

"I know you're not buying my bullshit, Skye."

I studied the man sitting in front of me, looking into his confident eyes. They told me he knew exactly what he was saying.

And I realised in that moment that he was reading me.

"What?" I managed to reply, as casually and nonchalantly as humanly possible. But the man sitting across from me did not blink an eye.

"It's very easy, Skye. It's all in your eyes."

My eyes?!

No, this is bullshit!

I never give it away!

Nobody had ever been able to read me as well as the stranger sitting in front of me in that moment, and it was a very bizarre feeling. For a second, a split second, the person in front of me didn't feel like a stranger at all.

No one's ever read me like this. No men I have ever dated, no friends of nearly two decades - not even my own parents.

And I began to tremble.

In fear.

In confusion.

In the inability to know how to react when someone is reading you this well.

"You're happy to be here, that's why you got a second drink. But you're even happier that soon you'll be able to walk out that door and win. You can't wait to see me lose."

*He's guessing, he doesn't know **for sure** Skye, there's*

just no way! Laugh it off, pretend he's got it all wrong! You can still win!

But I was too stunned to reply, too shocked to laugh it off and pretend he wasn't reading me. Because he was. I could see it. I could see it and feel it and there was no way of stopping it. It was like a bucket of water was being tipped on my head and all I could do was remain completely still. If I moved, if I showed any sort of emotion, he would win. He would win there and then. I couldn't let that happen.

"When I came back from my cigarette your phone was upside down on the table, which means you probably text a friend to update them, and you didn't want me to accidentally read their reply, as it's probably something like 'haha, so when are you leaving?!'

You went to the bathroom and didn't re-touch your lipstick, which means you probably don't want to kiss me tonight. Your body language - the crossed legs, the playing with your drink. You may be smiling and engaging in conversation with me very well, laughing at my jokes, but your eyes are telling me *'fuck you, you arrogant asshole. You're interesting, but you're not going to win this one'*.

Your innocent look doesn't fool me, Skye. It's funny because this has never happened before – somebody not buying the crap I say on first dates. It seems we can both read each other. And we're a dangerous combination – we both want to win. But at the end of the day Skye, somebody always has to lose."

Oh shit, I thought as I put down my wine glass.

I'm going to fall in love with this bastard.

Strangers

As he told me about the record label he had started at 18, I couldn't stop studying him, every inch of him. The way he moved his hands as he spoke, the way he stared down at his phone when he was distracted by my lips or by my hair or by anything about me. He had my attention now. There was something about him that now demanded my full attention.

I could tell he wanted to reach over the table and kiss me, but it wasn't the same for me, not at that stage. I was too distracted by how interesting he was, how captivating he was. I just wanted him to keep talking and never shut up, never stop telling me about his life, his goals, his thoughts.

In front of me sat a very intelligent, charismatic and funny man, and for only the second time in my life, looks took second place. What truly drew me in were the words and thoughts coming out of his mouth. I could see glimpses of his dark side even then, and he kept repeating *'I'm a fucking bastard when I want to be'* to warn me. I knew his callous side was the reason he was successful in his job and the smarter thing to do would be to walk away, but it was already too late. He had pulled me in, and now all I wanted to do was learn more about him.

His bad qualities shone through just as much as his good ones did, and I was in full acknowledgement that the person sitting in front of me was ruthless. You could tell he was the type of person that wouldn't even change expression if a girl began crying her eyes out in front of him.

There was this look in his eyes on that first date, as if he was so sure how this game was going to play out. It was a look as if I were only a conquest, that the following Saturday night would be another girl, another challenge. When he talked about himself the dialogue seemed well rehearsed and overused, girl after girl after girl...

An hour had passed since his speech about being able to read me; the speech that had completely thrown me off and yet simultaneously pulled me in. But after that he had gone back to bullshitting me. I didn't understand it, it frustrated me, yet I hadn't got up and left. I hadn't told him to fuck off. He knew I knew it was bullshit, that everything he was saying to me was to *sell*, to get what he wanted, but it seemed this was the only way he knew how to communicate with another person.

He didn't seem drawn in by me at all; it was a fake, sugar-coated persona he put on to score. I knew all of this and yet I was still there. I was still asking about him, still wanting to know more. He led an interesting life; a successful job, a nice flat in Notting hill, and he was obsessed with everything creative, just like me.

"I don't do relationships," he told me, as he looked down at the ice in his whiskey. I had heard it said time and time again by many men and women I knew, and I had always been able to detect their insincerity. Sometimes they were only lying to me, but other times they were lying to themselves too. The man sitting across from me that night however, was being completely and utterly truthful; he had never been in a relationship, and he was perfectly content.

In that respect, we were similar. I, too, did not wake up in the morning wanting or craving a relationship. Nevertheless, my reaction to feeling this way was a little different to his. The sad truth was that I didn't like a man very often. I dated them, sure, I cared about them, sure, but to really capture my attention or fall in love took a certain level of 'weirdness', or uniqueness. I couldn't explain it. And anyway, I was by no means an expert on what I wanted from my dating life – I was still learning, and the one person I had ever felt anything for had been an odd yet charismatic bassist of a rock band. Our story had been epically romantic and intense, as most good romances are, but I had eventually left him when I could see that he was losing interest. He still sometimes found me on social media to like a selfie or two.

Since the bassist I had dated too many people, people I hadn't loved, eventually hurting them, and then spending nights crying over the pain I had caused. I was an overly empathetic person, always sharing everyone else's pain along with my own. I'd cry over how much of a bitch I was, truly believing I was worthless, and not understanding why others were drawn in by me, when I gave nothing back. When I had nothing to give. I couldn't take it anymore; I had no energy left to channel other peoples' pain.

And so I had decided a couple of months back to not get into a relationship until I was in love with the person. It was only fair.

So it was okay to be there that night, listening to the cocky Italian man tell me about his life, with a face that might as well have read 'DANGER: STEP AWAY FROM THIS ASSHOLE'.

It was okay, because I was never going to see him again.
It was okay, because, well, I never liked anyone.

Friday Night

"Wahoo!" I squealed for the third time in the space of a minute, passing Sofia her pint of beer. "You are the only girl I know that voluntarily orders beer at the bar!" I shouted over the loud, crappy commercial song playing in the background.

"So sexist, Skye!" we both laughed, and I clinked my wine glass with her pint. Sofia was my closest friend at work. She was, if we have to give it a name, my Work Wife. We became instantly friends during my first week at my job, bonding over our mutual love of ice skating and cycling.

"Can I buy you a drink?" asked pervy Dan, one of our colleagues, as he appeared next to us.

"We're good Dan, thanks!" I replied for the both of us.

"Pervy Dan thinks he's getting lucky tonight," I whispered to Sofia, once he was out of earshot.

"Don't call him that, Skye! He's not pervy, come on..."

Sofia was one of those sweet girls that were also slightly on the naïve side. She always saw the best in people, and it was actually one of the things I liked most about her. She also knew every detail about my dating life, including the fact that it was exactly six weeks since I had dumped the unbelievably hot model with no brain cells.

That, I have to say, had been lots of fun. To date a model, I mean. But it had turned boring surprisingly quick. As entertaining as it had been to enter a party and have every single pair of eyes turn to stare, it appeared I required some sort of intelligent conversation to keep the attraction there.

And as amusing as it had been to see 16-year-old me doing cartwheels next to us every time we were together, I knew I had to let it go. And so I did, via text, to which neither of us had thrown a fit, cried, or felt even a speckle of sadness. If only the dating game were always that easy.

"Are you ready to part-ay?!" wailed Kim, with a jug of some sort of bright pink cocktail in her hand. Kim also worked with us but she was slightly on the bitchy side. We weren't big fans of girls like that, Sofia and I, but we were friendly with her anyway.

We all worked in payroll for a recruitment company – something I had never, ever imagined for myself. In fact, if someone had told me a year ago where I would be in 365 days, I would have laughed until my stomach hurt.

I had previously worked in the music business for eight years. It had been my passion, it had given me the drive to survive anything, or so I thought. I had started at 16 with the college magazine, interviewing musicians and organising gigs to coincide with the release of articles. That then later on led me to radio and niche record labels. Unfortunately for me, the music business was more business than it was music, and over time it had eaten me up and spat me back out. Everyone had told me it was a tough industry to crack, but I guess you're never going to believe it until you see it for yourself. I survived as long as I could, but in my eighth year, my self-esteem was in tatters and I had no choice but to take a break.

And so I decided to take a step away from bands and backstage passes to make money whilst I thought what my next step would be. I would go back to music eventually, of course – that was where I belonged. But for now I was good, I had quickly come to like the people I worked with, and a new concept was growing on me – one of not having a goal, but instead enjoying the present moment. What was wrong with that? Nothing, if it made me feel good.

And it did.

"It's Friday night!" Sofia stated, in case we were unaware.

"Kim, is that cocktail big enough for you?" I asked jokily, nodding at her jug.

"Never big enough for me, darling!"

All three of us cackled and I took a gulp from my glass of wine, putting my arm around Sofia.

"You know, I look forward to this moment every week babe," I told her, as we moved away from the others.

"Skye, are you tipsy already?"

"*So* glad you said tipsy and not drunk."

"Yeah, yeah, I know...*Skye doesn't get drunk, she gets*

tipsy. You never get to the point that you are throwing up or pulling up your skirt for the bartender, *blah, blah, blah*...Heard the speech a million times before!"

"It's a skill, Sofia. It's a skill that very few people have."

Sofia playfully rolled her eyes at me, and took a gulp from her beer. She was going to need it if she was going to spend the night hanging out with tipsy me. I was a lot to handle, even sober. Imagine the havoc I unleashed when I had some wine in me.

"So, any guys? Update me," she ordered.

My Work Wife was in a 15-year relationship with a man called Alfie, one of the loveliest fellows I had ever met, but sometimes it felt as if Sofia lived vicariously through me. It's bizarre how people who have been in relationships a long time see the single life as an urban legend.

"None since the model," I told her.

"Will you see that arrogant guy again?"

I recalled Bastard-eyes sitting opposite me at that bar in Maiden Vale. He had been able to read me. I had been able to read him.

Had I thought about him? A little. Okay, a lot. But I hadn't text him. And he hadn't text me.

"No way!"

"Why, Skye? He sounded interesting. A bit full of himself, sure, but charming in his own way..."

Sofia's naivety shone through much more once she had some beer in her. I wanted to tell her that I felt powerless in his company, and that that wasn't something I looked for in a man, but I decided to leave it alone. It was a waste of time to talk about someone I was never going to see again.

"Not my type. And anyway, you and I sit next to each other! If I had any gossip I would tell you at work. So...let's instead drink up, and make it a good one!" We *woo*'d over the music for no reason at all, other than for the simple fact that life was good. It really was.

Bastard-eyes:

Hey Skye
How are you?
How has your week been?
I've been swamped with work.
It's crazy round here!
Ever been to a meeting where the client is super uncooperative?
Happened to me this morning, I really had to use my people skills to make him see sense…
Anyway, sorry I hadn't text sooner.
Hope you're having a good one…

Howls

I didn't understand how I had ended up at Bastard-eyes' Notting hill flat. It was our second date, a date I hadn't planned on ever letting happen, but somehow it had anyway, and consisted of dinner at his. It was going well so far. It had started off with that type of awkwardness you'd expect for two people who have only ever been on one date. An hour in and there I sat in the corner of his kitchen, watching him make lasagne.

He was again wearing a ridiculously expensive shirt, Armani this time, and I swear there was *even more* gel in his hair than on the first date, if that was even possible. He always seemed to look absolutely flawless and pristine, and his flat matched that. There was not a speck of dirt to be found. He gave me a quick tour when I first arrived and every single thing in his flat looked as if it had taken a good year to pick out. A good year! Everything was shiny and stylish and absolutely nothing like me or my style at all. I often looked tired and didn't straighten my hair properly, leaving one part accidentally curly, or putting on my eyeliner wrong or getting lipstick on my teeth. I was more boyish than I was girlish, and he was more girlish than he was boyish.

I was the last person you'd go to when you wanted to renovate your house or flat, and the last girl you'd go to when planning what to wear for, well, any occasion. I mean, look, I did alright – I wore sexy skirts on dates and elegant dresses at weddings, but they weren't the latest trend, and they weren't ridiculously expensive.

He was very into fashion and the latest trends, and had a piercing on his tongue that made me want to jump him. Also, call me crazy but he moved with far more poise than me.

"Skye, can you stir that pot for me?" he asked, snapping me out of my stare.

Me? No guy ever asks me to help out cooking when on a date.

Even whilst helping, my eyes were on him. I listened to him talk about his job, and watched his eyes light up as he spoke about struggle – any sort of struggle. His move to London, his problems at work, the arguments with his flatmate. He lived off of it, fed off of it. He was one of those people that needed obstacles in his life; it made the triumph that much more glorious.

And he was obsessed with powerful male TV characters. *Do you watch Suits? Have you seen Breaking Bad? What about House of Cards?*

I wondered about the last time I had succeeded at something, and my heart sank. I hadn't won in a while. A long while. Struggle? Challenge? These were not words currently in my vocabulary. Success didn't seem like something for me, not right now, and I was okay with that. I had to be.

He was still his bullshitter self; skirting around the details of his life, but God forbid he reveal anything personal about himself. He was still very much all about *selling*. I wanted the 'real' him to show its face again, but I wondered if that would ever happen.

"Have you ever been to New York, Skye?" he asked me, as he fiddled with some lasagne sheets. It was the first time that evening that he had asked me a single question about myself.

"No, it's my dream to go – since I was 10. It's on the list."

"What are you waiting for?!"

"I actually have dreams about New York at least once every six months, each dream different from the last."

He frowned.

"Yeah, it's pretty weird. I guess *you* have been there?"

"Oh yes, I love New York. I try to go out there as often as possible. Maybe some time we can go together? I'm going in August."

When a person I hardly knew said this sort of crap it really irritated me. It was such a bullshitter thing to say. Usually men said it primarily to get you into bed, however with Bastard-eyes I wondered if it was a combination of both hoping to score, but also a certain curiosity to see my reaction.

He seemed the type of person who liked to study the behavior of others. He had said something similar on our first date too – when I mentioned I wanted to go to Tokyo, he suggested we go together. Is that really something you say to someone on a first date?

Maybe I was just seeing what I wanted to see, but it seemed like there was more to his behavior, that it wasn't just about playing the game; that he liked to test people.

And I answered him the same way I did all bullshitters – by playing along.

"Why not?! Would be fun!"

You bullshitting asshole, remind me again why I'm here?

Because Sofia is away with Alfie this weekend Skye, and you have nothing better to do.

Once we sat down it was still pretty awkward between us, and he began asking me about my travels.

"You recently went to Barcelona, right?" he queried, as he sat himself down opposite me at the glass dining table. "How was it?"

"It was wonderful, have you ever been?"

"No, but it's on the list."

"Oh you simply must go-" I suddenly heard a howl. It sounded like a fox. I briefly peered through his window down to his garden, but it was pitch black and nothing could be seen. I looked back at the man sitting across from me. He had no reaction to the howl and I decided he had probably not heard it.

"Yes, you simply must go, it's beautiful!"

Another howl.

"So what did you see? Did you have any adventures?"

"I did indeed!"

Another howl.

"For example, on the first morning I decided to go for a jog along the beach and there was this old man-"

Another howl.

"Are they having sex?!" I blurted out.

The man froze, a forkful of lasagne just inches from his lips. "*Who?* You and the old man?!"

I blushed. I blushed worse than I had done in a long time. "No! The foxes! The foxes outside! Can't you hear them?"

The man laughed, sighing in relief. "Oh! Skye. For a second I thought you had sex on the beach with this old man…"

We both laughed hysterically, dropping our forks at the same time, as our laughter took over. I looked at him – the bullshitter was gone. The man who had sat opposite me at that bar in Maiden Vale telling me he could read me was back.

Stay this time! I much prefer you!

"I was thinking geez, she's a keen one, isn't she?!" we laughed some more, our eyes fixed on one another as we did so, completely dissolving any awkwardness between us. My stomach ached from all the laughter. "Oh God Skye, that was too funny."

And just like that, he stopped selling.

Bastard-eyes:

Skye, I wanna see you again.
What are you doing this Saturday?
Shall we go for dinner?
Outside this time…
I know the perfect little place ☺

A woman of quality learns the art of balancing between the right proportion of *if I want to kiss him I will* and *I do not chase: I am chased.*

Bernard

It was exactly a week later that I awkwardly stood at the door of the man's bedroom. His bedroom was precisely how I had imagined it – vinyl collection on a shelf, his work piled on a black leather sofa, and a massive David Bowie poster of his 1977 album 'Low'. He liked controversial styles and people; the ones that thought outside the box. He said life was too boring to let it ever become monetising, even with the people in your inner circle. I still didn't understand anything about fashion, and being around him I was constantly reminded of how little feminine I truly was.

We had been texting all week, back and forth. On our second date the previous Saturday night I had stayed until 4:45AM. Believe it or not, we had stayed up all night talking. About work, about goals, about striving for what you want. Well, he had done most of the talking, and I had listened. He had gone to the army for a year to carry on the family tradition, and to make his dad happy. He had then returned home and with all his might had stood before his parents and said, 'father, I want to have a career. A different career to the one you want for me. I hope you will accept this'. I could imagine his gracious tone, his curious eyes, as he told his parents this. When he spoke about his folks there was less arrogance in his tone. In fact, he almost appeared humble. Almost.

It seemed he got on with his father but that he was much closer to his mother, and I do mean *much* closer. He told her everything. She even knew about me, which I found slightly weird.

We had stayed in his kitchen until the early hours of the morning; drinking wine, laughing at the smallest of things, and telling stories. It actually terrified me how much I enjoyed his company and how well I was able to communicate with him. Our conversation simply flowed, and continued to do so, hour after hour. I just never wanted it to end. He was interested in me now, no longer putting on a façade to try and score. And so now I wanted him to kiss me, I did. It didn't seem logical, neither of us wanted or were capable of having a relationship, so it would simply be sex, and I was old enough to know that nothing is ever just sex.

I eyed his king-sized bed in front of me, and just as every time you first encounter the bed of the person you are dating, it was instantly the elephant in the room. It was as if it were looking at me, shaking its eyebrows at me. *'You're going to be using me later'*, it smarmed in a perverse tone. Bernard the bed, that's what I called him. No matter where I went, his name was always Bernard.

No, I always replied. *We don't know that yet. I can always say no. And anyway, perhaps he brought me up here to talk about the possibility of Brexit or the current status of the UK trading market...*

"It's a bit messy, sorry – I usually clean up on Sundays," he told me, as he moved a couple of shirts off his bed. Yet again, his entire flat was completely and utterly spotless; he was clearly lying and had spent the majority of his Saturday cleaning.

Ha, he should see my place.

He grabbed his laptop and sat himself down on the leather sofa. I slowly went and placed myself in the opposite corner.

"Let me show you some of the awards I've won in the past," he peered over at me, and slapped his hand on the leather cushion. "Come here! What are you doing all the way over there?!"

I awkwardly slid over and we turned our attention to his laptop.

"So if we look over at..."

I drifted off into thought as he spoke about his career. He seemed to be becoming more self-centered and arrogant with every passing moment. *Why would anyone want him by their side?* I asked myself.

But sitting next to him, the hairs on the back of my neck instantly stood up. He was egotistical, yes, but somehow he was also interesting. I didn't understand it.

I *couldn't* understand it.

"...then I worked for a really famous artist..." he named some guy and asked me if I knew him. I didn't. He lost himself in conversation about this person, and I lost myself in his eyes.

How are they pulling me in like this?

They were big and brown and curious. Sure, they were bastard eyes, but, it seemed like there was more to them. I saw coldness, but also some sort of hidden warmth. Yet I told myself I was simply seeing what I wanted to see. *The man sitting next to me is clearly a cold bastard, remember this Skye.*

Nonetheless, I hadn't cancelled the date, I hadn't left after dinner, and I had yet to leave that sofa.

It didn't make any sense.

I can leave whenever I want.

Whenever I want.

He suddenly looked at my lips as he spoke and it brought me back to reality.

Does he want to kiss me?!

Do it! Do it! Kiss me!

His eyes suddenly looked up to meet mine, and then back at the laptop. Again he started talking about his bloody awards, but I wasn't listening. I was waiting for him to take his eyes off that damn laptop and look at me, because I knew when he would, they would drop to my lips. And I was waiting for that. Yearning for that. I was ready.

It took a good minute for him to turn back to me, and again he looked at my lips, this time keeping his eyes fixed on them, and I was sure he was going to lean in, but he didn't. He didn't and again his eyes went back to the laptop as he continued to talk.

What the hell was that?! Does he not want to kiss me?! Am I not attractive enough?! Has he decided he doesn't want to kiss me? Is he waiting for me to leave-

He suddenly turned to me, and leaned in. I did the same, and we paused just inches from each other's lips for a moment, a brief moment, as my heart began to race.

Wait for it.

Wait for it.

He couldn't hold back any longer and he kissed me,

passionately, putting a hand on my neck, authoritatively.

I returned the passion, grabbing his face with both my hands, as everything else in the world fell to pieces. I didn't understand what was happening. It was as if in three seconds the world had just completely turned upside down. And most bizarre of all was that it felt as if we had never gone a moment without kissing, without exploring each other's bodies. It felt as if we already knew each other, when in reality this was only our third date, only the third time we were in each other's company, and the first time our bodies were learning of one another. It was the most powerful, most exhilarating first kiss I had ever experienced. I pounced at him, leaping onto his lap as we continued to kiss.

I could faintly hear Bernard muttering to himself behind us.

"Hey, I thought you were going to use me first? Inconsiderate assholes."

Mondays

I strolled into work on Monday morning with a massive grin on my face, and a certain swagger to my walk. I smiled at everyone on the tube, I waited for old ladies at traffic lights to help them cross the road, and I said hello to the homeless man outside the work building (ignoring his very fowl response).

"You had sex!" Sofia wailed, pointing her finger at me as I arrived at our joint desks.

"Good morning to you too, lovely!"

"You had sex! I'm not sure with who, where, if it was good, but…you banged someone!"

A few people in the office looked our way and I ssh'd my enthusiastic Work Wife. "Keep it down, will you? Yes, I did."

"With who? Did you go back to the model? I knew you would, he was too hot."

"No! God no. With the arrogant guy."

"Bastard-eyes?"

"Not calling him that anymore. But yes – with Bastard-eyes."

"Ooh, how was it?" she whispered, enjoying the scandal element to our Monday morning conversation. "I thought he was a massive asshole and you were never going to see him again?"

"I wasn't. But then I did. It was…Sofia…" I lowered my voice. "It was amazing, but, more than the sex…it was us hanging out – I liked it a lot. I was surprised. We spent the entire weekend in bed, talking, laughing, watching films, TV shows, adverts."

"Adverts?"

"Yes, we're both weird and love to analyse adverts."

Sofia cocked up an eyebrow, but shook it off, more interested in other details.

"So you gonna see him again? Was he less cold with you this time?"

"I think so. And no, he actually did something weird – apart from no cuddles whatsoever, I put a hand on his chest at one point whilst we were talking about something or other, and he moved it away!"

"*What? Why?*"

"I don't know! It seemed it was too intimate for him. We slept on completely separate sides of his bed, and he was not selling or bullshitting, but he was very far away. *Very* far away. Like he wasn't in that bed with me. Like I was alone." My tone had suddenly turned morose, and the smile on my face disappeared.

"Hmm, be careful, Skye. What horoscope is he?"

I wanted to roll my eyes – I didn't believe in horoscopes, but I knew if I did it would hurt Sofia. "Cancer."

"Ooh, cancers are very to themselves, Skye. Very stubborn. And very attached to their mothers, is he attached to his mother?"

"Yes," I told her, unable to shake the feeling of how alone I had felt in that bed. Especially when he had moved my hand away, so casually, as he had spoken. As he had smiled. As he had lived on a completely different planet to mine.

"Let's check out his horoscope's plans this week, shall we," Sofia told me, as she opened up the newspaper.

The World's Biggest Pizzas

Whilst getting ready to see him the following Saturday night, I made a promise to myself. I promised to be just as cold with him as he were with me. I promised myself that if I felt unhappy or uncomfortable acting that way, that I would never see him again.

When I arrived at his place, I found that he had already cooked dinner – mushroom risotto.

"Come on, let's go eat it in bed."

I frowned. I hadn't pegged him as an eating-in-bed kind of guy – he looked too neat and tidy and control freak for that. But clearly I was wrong.

After much debate over what to watch, we somehow ended up choosing a documentary on the world's biggest pizzas. We sat crossed legged on his bed, laughing and shouting at the TV as we ate.

"Oh come on, that pizza is insane!" he wailed, and I watched him with a smile. He seemed more relaxed than usual.

Don't forget your promise, Skye.

I snapped out of my gaze and focused back on the documentary. Once we finished, he gently took my plate from me and put them both in the kitchen. When he came back I was lying on my back, laughing at the massive pizza being carried across a small town in South Italy.

"Hey, what did I miss?" he crawled into the bed next to me, and lay on his back beside me.

"Well they tried to carry it across the town but it's not easy..."

"Of course it's not easy, the pizza is the same damn size as the town!"

"But if they surely used a forklift..." my voice died away, as I felt his hand suddenly graciously place itself on top of mine.

What is he doing?

He began rubbing circles on my knuckles as he laughed, his eyes fixed on the TV.

"It's gonna break!"

28

"It is," I replied as casually as possibly, even though at this point I was trembling. I didn't understand what was happening. Why was he being affectionate? This was a first, and I didn't know how to react, but I liked it. I liked it a lot. It was so soothing, so therapeutic, and my promise to remain cold melted in the space of three seconds.

"Look at him! The 'genius' chef, but he didn't think how to then carry it across town, did he?" he told me, as he continued to rub circles, but I was no longer able to concentrate on the documentary. I was mesmerised by what was happening; never had I been more drawn in by someone's affection. It was so little, so minor on the spectrum of human affection, and yet it felt like so much. Half because I knew it was difficult for him to do, and half because, well, it was from him.

And that seemed to mean something to me.

Lone Wolf

"Laugh at his joke!' the man hissed only loud enough for me to hear, as he elbowed me gently in the stomach. I instantly let out the loudest, most fake laugh imaginable. All heads at the restaurant table turned to look at me, bewildered looks on their faces. My partner in crime covered his face with his hand, trying his hardest not to laugh.

The first time he took me to a business dinner I think I was already in over my head. It had taken me 0.5 seconds to fall for his brilliance. I was getting attached, to both him and his crazy world, to a land where life ran at 100 mph. One night he would be in London having sushi with me, the next he would be in Rome leading a conference, calling me from his hotel balcony as he smoked his eighteenth cigarette.

But when he started taking me with him to these dinners he wasn't taking me as something on his arm, as most of his colleagues did. He was taking me as Skye – *girl with a brain, girl with something to say.* He hid behind the mask of a superficial twat in a Dolce & Gabbana suit, but underneath, he had more depth than I could ever have imagined. Every day I was learning something new about him. Just that morning I had discovered his undying love for art – he would spend hour after hour staring at a painting, or musing over a drawing. When you would ask him about it he would tell you a zillion different things about the piece, from the texture to the style to the artist's hometown and his/her influences. He was an encyclopedia of knowledge on art, and each day something else about him was revealed, each fact more surprising than the last.

Being the lone wolf that he was, he had never taken anyone with him to these dinners, but he had started doing so with me to teach me exactly how to play the game at these sorts of events. Because I was far from good at these things. Because I was not a natural people person. I was awkward and weird, and I couldn't be fake. As a kid when I would go to birthday parties I would sit in the corner and cry. I had mentioned this to him one night and a few days later, he was adamant I be at that business dinner.

But two hours had passed and I was still as tense as when I had first walked through the door.

He, on the other hand, was by far the best talker at that table. Which made sense, since he couldn't ever bear to be second place in anything. He was very competitive, and of course, his arrogance made sure to always be present too. These qualities half put me off and half made me want to run into his arms.

We were seeing each other a few nights a week now, but we were not official in any way, shape or form. What did that mean? It meant he could see whoever he wanted to, and so could I. Except I wasn't. I was only seeing him. He never spoke about other girls but I knew he was seeing them. He would sometimes take hours to reply to a text, or upload a particularly handsome picture of himself and I'd know it wasn't for me. But I was okay with it. I had to be. I was so drawn in by him that my sole goal was to get to know him better; nothing else seemed to matter.

Once attendance at these business dinners became a regular occurrence for me, I always seemed to find myself studying him; the way he spoke to people, pulled them in. And his jokes, oh his jokes! I often feared his humour was going to cause serious damage to my stomach. All eyes at the table would be fixated on him, admiring him, holding onto his every word. It wasn't his appearance that drew you in, no – it was only once he opened his mouth that he captured your attention; anyone could dress up in a sharp suit and put too much gel in their hair. He instead captivated you with what he had to say, of how he said it, of what he could teach you.

As time went on I began to relax at these things, and slowly but surely I started to become good at 'playing the game'. We would high five each other under the table when I would help him reel in a new client. And he would text me saying, 'going well, right?' when he would slip outside for a cigarette. 'If he hits on you while I'm out here tell me, he was looking at you funny'.

When we were at those dinners, his hand on my thigh as he told a story, it was then that I was at my happiest. We were one. We were a team. Nobody could beat us.

And for a moment, a brief moment, I forgot the other girls. I forgot his coldness. All I saw were two people that worked well together, that had each other's backs.

Two people that were seamlessly content simply being in each other's company.

Our hearts are like children: you assume they will listen to what you have to say, but they never do. They do what they want and only come back to you when they are in trouble.

The Question

I was completely uninspired by life and the goals you should set yourself, I had been for a long time. I had accepted that my life would steer in whichever direction it wanted to, that I was not in charge. I had spent eight years in the music business, and where had it got me?

Eight years of my dreams being the driving force of my entire life, and what exactly had I achieved in that time?

Nothing.

So I was okay playing it safe; never taking risks, never fighting for what I wanted. I didn't seem to gain either way, so why even try?

But he was a fighter, and his way of life quickly began to make me question my own choices, my own attitude towards life.

I started crying out of nowhere. We were in his kitchen, and as always, he was gloating about success at work that day as we cooked dinner. Suddenly I had tears in my eyes, and they wouldn't stop coming.

"Skye?"

I went and sat down on a chair, trying to stop but failing miserably. In fact, it seemed the more I tried to stop crying, the more tears that rolled down my cheeks. They were multiplying. The man rushed over and kneeled down in front of me.

"Leave me! I'm fine!" was my response, of course. Women – we make no sense. I hid my face with the kitchen towel – I didn't like people seeing me cry; it showed weakness. But he was stronger than me and he yanked the towel away from my face, putting his hands on both my cheeks to make sure he was looking me straight in the eye.

"What is it?" he asked, in the most serious tone I had ever heard him use in the two months I had been seeing him.

"I don't know! What am I doing with my life? Where did my goals go? My dreams? I'm living for the weekend? When did I become that girl?"

"You're not that girl, Skye. You just took a break. Relax, you're back. Welcome back to the jungle. It's hell here, but it's also beautiful. Don't lose focus, tell me what you want to do." The arrogant twat was nowhere in sight; the pair of eyes in front of me seemed almost human.

"I don't know." What a puddle of pathetic I had become. Crying in the kitchen of a man who had his shit together. Crying in the kitchen of a man who was not even my boyfriend. I was most certainly not looking for answers from him; I could handle this alone.

"Yes you do, concentrate. What do you want to do?"

"I. Don't. Know!" Our dinner was overcooking – I could see the smoke from the corner of my blurred eyes. I knew he could see it too, yet he wouldn't leave my side. We could smell it burning, but he was concentrating so hard on me that I wasn't sure he even cared if his flat went up in flames.

For the first time in a long time, I was scared. Terrified, in fact. At the reality that I had no idea what I wanted to do with my life, or perhaps, it was more the realisation that I actually *wanted* something for myself. All that telling myself I was happy doing nothing was complete and utter bullshit. I was a person that needed a reason to get up in the morning. I was a person that needed ambition and drive. It was just that the music business had messed me around for far too many years, and to think there was a possibility I may have to let go of that dream had been hard. To accept that perhaps my future didn't lie in music had been brutal; it had left me feeling unworthy of any ambition, of any drive.

Why should I have any of that when it's futile?

I had been rejected by the industry. I had failed. *So why should I start again, only to fail again?*

I continued to cry as he rubbed my back. This was the most intimate the man had ever been with me, and I wanted to appreciate the moment, I really did, but I was too filled with sadness to do so. The frustration, the fear – it was all there now, coming out in my tears. I had had no idea that I felt this way until that moment. And it felt as if I were having an out-of-body experience, watching myself cry and asking, 'why is that girl crying? What's wrong with her?'

The man stayed by my side as I sobbed, and we both let our dinner burn to a crisp.

Sofia:

So when are you going to invite him out with us?

Skye:

He's not really a social person – he works a lot.

Sofia:

Oh gosh, can you imagine being that lonely? I wouldn't be able to do it

Skye:

Yeah but he's at least working towards a goal, right?

Sofia:

I guess.

Sofia:

Though I much prefer drinking towards a goal!
Hahaha

Determination

Panic took over and I couldn't breathe.

"...but I'm sure you'll get there eventually, right? Everyone does," said the cocky asshole sitting opposite me. He smiled smugly at me. It was punches to the stomach hearing his insults, and looking into his belittling eyes. I watched as he dabbed his mouth with his napkin, and his eyes slowly passed over to the man, who sat next to me. "What?" The cocky asshole uttered to the man, who was staring back at him in fury.

"Excuse me," I managed to say as I pushed back my chair, and walked out of the five-star restaurant as casually as possible. In a way that didn't reveal how close to tears I was or the fact that I was having trouble breathing. I took a right outside the restaurant and turned into a dark alley. I leaned my head back against the cold wall and closed my eyes.

My stomach was somersaulting with nerves, and my head pounding with toxic, insecure thoughts.

I can't do this, I can't do this, I can't do this. No one thinks I can, because they know I can't. Who the fuck am I kidding? Trying to find myself? Me? A people person? Me? They're all laughing at me. They know the truth. The truth that I couldn't see. Or I refused to see. But now I can, and they're right! I can't do this. I just can't.

"Hey," said a voice. It was a calming, familiar voice. I opened my eyes to see the man standing in front of me, looking at me with concerned eyes.

The last person I want to see right now, I said to myself. *With his success and confidence and brilliance! Next to him I am a joke, a failure, a kid...*

"I don't want to talk about it-" I tried to leave and make my way back to the restaurant, but he put a warm and gentle hand on my forearm.

"Skye, wait a minute," he said, authoritatively.

There he is again with his calm tone. Can't he understand how upsetting this is? To be humiliated in there by those snobs? Looked down upon? No, he can't. Because he's a bastard, just like them. He is hard, just like them. He knows how to destroy the people in there. I don't. And that's a certified distinction between us.

"Look, I-"

"Skye."

I sighed. "Fine." I leaned my head back against the wall. He put a hand on my cheek delicately, as if I were fragile. I, in turn, looked anywhere but at him. I was ashamed. I had thought I could become a stronger person, that perhaps I could belong in the world of chasing your dreams. But now I knew this wasn't the case. I had been looking forward to this dinner all week; around that table sat the CEOs of some of the biggest record labels in London, brought together by the man currently caressing my cheek.

After my meltdown in his kitchen, he felt he needed to help me find new inspiration, but I was beginning to feel a lot like a charity case. It was futile for me to have hopes and dreams. I was weak and I would never survive.

"Skye, look at me."

I slowly obeyed, finding I was too low on energy and morale to fight him. When I did so I was met by his powerful brown eyes, they looked back at me with undivided attention. I wondered what he saw when he looked at me.

A joke.

"You are better than all of them in there," he told me, and I forced a laugh.

"Oh really? Which one in particular? The one with the villa in the Canary Islands, or the one with the-"

"They are very successful people, yes. But you know how they got there, Skye? A brilliant mind, and perseverance. You have both." It was said as if it were plain fact. There was not an ounce of doubt in his tone. "Skye, listen to me. You are powerful. You are just not channeling that power yet. You will. And you are going to be brilliant. I can see it. I know it."

The man had my full attention now. My anxiety began to melt away, replaced by curiosity. My eyes were fixed on his, as if he were somehow passing me some of his strength.

He truly believed in me, but it was the first time I was

actually seeing it. Never had I had someone believe in me so strongly, so fiercely, as if my strength were the most obvious thing in the world.

And never had such belief channeled such power before, I could feel it.

"Close your eyes," he ordered in a softer tone. Once again, I obeyed. "I shouldn't have to tell you this, your strength should come from within, but... I guess because you've been out of the game a while you need to be reminded. Skye, you are incredibly intelligent, interesting, beautiful, and amazing to be around. You can easily knock that bastard off his high horse playing the same tricks he is. If that's what you want to do. You've got it in you.

Alternatively, if you prefer, we could say we have to go home and then get a takeaway on the way..."

I opened my eyes. I felt stronger because of his words, I did. I felt more alive than I had done in a long time. But I was also terrified. Of failure. Of humiliation. And that fear, it was stronger than my drive.

"Can we get a takeaway?" As soon as I said it I felt like the biggest coward in the world, but that didn't make me open my mouth and change my mind.

"Sure, Skye. Of course. We can get your favourite chocolate cake, too."

We choose to put our hearts at risk for the ones we think are worth it. We must or we may never love.

The Bio

"Ready?" he asked.

"Hmm."

He switched off the light, and crawled into the king-sized bed next to me. This was our routine: after dinner we would watch something in bed with chocolate biscuits, until one of us would begin to fall asleep. Then we would brush our teeth, change into our pyjamas, and get into bed. He always gave me a playful shove as we brushed our teeth in front of the mirror, and I always stuck my tongue out at him as we changed. His bathroom was ransacked with tons of medicine and crap that belonged to his flatmate, Tommaso, someone I never saw for more than ten seconds at a time. He didn't seem to spend a lot of time at home. All I knew was that he was a hotshot director of some big marketing company and that he hated onions.

After changing into our pyjamas, I would crawl into bed whilst he went to check the front door was locked for the fifth time. He was nervous about that sort of thing.

I usually wore his favourite American basketball shirt – no idea who the team were, I only cared that it smelled of him. Since he never cuddled me at night I needed some sort of substitution. And so I would fall asleep breathing in his scent, imagining his arms around me.

He still wasn't a big 'toucher'. He'd kiss me a lot, especially as we cooked dinner or at breakfast, but he wouldn't spoon me. He was someone who liked to be left alone on his side of the bed. This was hard for me, as I was a very affectionate person, but I respected his wants and needs, not keen on seeming needy or desperate for his affection. But in reality, I was.

He had however bought me a pillow. Before we met and during the first month that we were seeing each other, he had only owned one pillow. This was so that no one could ever stay the night, at least not on a weekly basis. I never said anything about it, but in my head I kept thinking: This guy is nuts. Who goes to such lengths to make sure nobody enters your life on a permanent basis?

But once we started seeing each other a few times a week, I went over one night and there it was. I never said a word to him, I didn't want to be the girl that prompted the guy she liked to go and buy a pillow for her. No way. If he wanted to go get one he would, and sure enough he did. When I came over he was so excited to show me it, so adamant that I place my head on it to check if it was comfortable enough for me, soft enough for me. It was hard not to laugh at how enthusiastic he really was over it, and the fact that he spent a whole 30 minutes talking about a damn pillow. But I refrained from giggling – the truth was it was nice to see him excited about something other than work.

"Goodnight," I said to him, turning to my side.

"Goodnight."

I hugged myself in his basketball shirt, taking in his scent and starting to drift off into my world; a world where he had his arms wrapped around me...

"Oh, hey, before I forget, I wanted to ask you something," he suddenly said.

Puzzled, I snapped out of my fantasy and turned back around to face him. I could vaguely see the outline of his face in the darkness of his room.

"What's up?"

"Can you write my bio for me? For my website. I need a bio."

I raised an eyebrow in intrigue. "Your bio?"

"Yes. I need one done."

"Why me?" I blurted out. "I haven't written anything in years..." *And you could easily hire an actual writer.*

"Because you know me," he replied. "Make me look like an asshole."

"That won't be hard."

"But, this is a business deal; no feelings involved. I'm gonna pay you, and you have a deadline. You don't reach it, you're fired. Oh, and I want nothing but the best, remember this will be read by people at the top. Make me look good. Okay?"

"Erm, yeah. Sure." *Wait, why did I just agree to that?*

Do I want to write his bio?
Am I even capable of writing his bio?! He has quite the impressive career, but he'll be fussy with the style, the details I put in...
Do I really want to do this?
The next day I sat down and opened up my laptop, staring at the blank page. It seemed quite ridiculous – hiring me to write about him. He could easily hire someone professional to do this for him. Yet I hadn't told him no. I hadn't called the idea ludicrous or laughed in his face. And I realised, a part of me wanted to do this, to take on this challenge.

But instead of starting work on it, I decided to check social media. I then decided to text some friends I hadn't spoken to in a while, and sing along to some classic Rolling Stones songs.

I did everything I could to avoid writing.

Once I eventually began however, a mere four hours later, I couldn't stop. I had the bio done in three hours. I read over it and liked what I had written. But decided I could do better.

And so I opened a new document, and wrote another one. I did this about five times before I was left with a bio I was actually happy with. With a quality of writing I was satisfied with. I was both surprised and impressed at what I had been able to achieve with a little focus. And just how much I enjoyed writing. To me writing was therapeutic; a natural part of my life. But somewhere along the way, and I couldn't remember where exactly, I had given up on it.

I sent it to him and after a couple more drafts, he absolutely loved it, and so did I. Other people started asking me to write their bios, hiring me for other writing jobs, and I began to get a strange feeling.

At first I couldn't understand what it was exactly.

But eventually I realised that it was a feeling of fulfilment.

I had forgotten just how much I liked to write.

And it seemed I wasn't half bad at it, either.

The Shark

Every single morning he would set the alarm for 6AM, and when it would go off he would be up like a shot. He used to say, 'as soon as my feet hit the floor that's it, I'm ready for another day battling the world'.

"Come on baby, up!"

The girl sleeping next to him, who frequently had dreams about chocolate and laughed when she saw people jogging, found this new lifestyle extremely hard to adjust to. She had never dated someone with such incredible discipline, and she spent the first few months having nothing to do with it, pretending it didn't exist. Once they started to get a little closer however, he convinced her to try the morning runs with him to help with her new hobby - boxing.

At first she would kick and scream when the alarm would go off, call him every name under the sun, or pretend to still be asleep. But with his demanding character, her sly plans to escape were always defeated. And as time went by, she began to resist less.

A few months into their new routine, he came back one night upset over having not won an award he had really wanted. The next morning when his phone alarm sounded, the girl saw an arm shoot out from underneath the blanket, switch it off and then disappear again. Curiously, she slowly got up and looked at him. His eyes were closed shut.

"Come on, time to get up!" she told him.

"Not today," were the only two words he uttered, and they were two words she had never heard him say before.

"Not a choice. Go hard or go home, remember?" Silence. "Up, up, up! Come on!" After pushing him out of bed, he eventually gave in and got changed. But he didn't say anything as he got dressed, or as they made their way out, or even as they walked to the park.

"I don't want to run today Skye, I told you," he finally said, as soon as they entered Holland park. He stopped. "I'm going home," he turned around, but the girl jumped out in front of him, blocking his way.

"Wait!" she shrieked, shoving a palm in his face. "You're here now. You can't leave me to run here alone anyway - look!" she pointed at a thirty-something man passing them; his eyes were looking straight ahead, oblivious to them. "Did you see that? City Slicker was checking out my ass, did you see that?! You gonna leave me alone here with him?! As he listens to Pitbull and checks out my ass?!"

"Skye-"

"You just gonna give up?" the girl asked in a more serious tone, studying the man standing in front of her. Never had she seen such weakness in his eyes. Never had she connected with his pain like this before. There was more to the story than she knew. He was cold for a reason. His pain was a black hole, and it was swallowing him up. Never had she wanted to help another person so much as she did him in that moment; to pull him out, to save him from himself. "Are you a fighter or a doormat?"

"I just need to go back to the flat-"

"So you're a doormat." Silence. "I don't like doormats; I like fighters. He's in there somewhere." Silence. "You know, I hated their review of you, they made you sound like…like…" she hesitated. "…canned tuna! Yes, canned tuna. You never have been and never will be canned tuna, remember this."

He gulped, as he listened to her. The girl didn't recognise herself or the strength she was currently emanating, but she liked it. She liked that her words were having an effect on him. She had his total attention, and he was taking in every word.

"You are a shark. You go after the people that think they can beat you, and you eat them alive. Not winning that award? That should only push you even more to win the next one."

He continued to stare at her.

"You are the strongest person I know, and there is no room here for self-doubt. No room. Because there is not an ounce of reservation. You are a Shark."

She got out her phone and headphones, putting one in each of his ears.

"Now, to remind you of the Harvey Spectre that you are, you are going to listen to the Suits soundtrack as you run and get out some of that anger and frustration in this park. Then, we're gonna go home and you're gonna get back to work and I'm gonna work on that bio for Sara.

Then tonight we will re-evaluate when you take me to dinner and tell me how pretty I look in my dress."

For the first time in nearly 24 hours, his eyes suddenly smiled ever so slightly.

"What are you waiting for?" she told him in a strict tone. As if in a trance, he gently took her phone into his hands.

"Let me know if City Slicker comes back," the Shark told the girl, before jogging off into the distance.

"Thank you," he whispered.

"Why are you thanking me?" the girl asked, confused.

"Because I am happy."

The Definition

When the girl arrived at the Shark's flat to find the kitchen covered in rose-scented candles, she thought he must have had a stroke. Candles and the Shark didn't really make a likely pairing. He was far too cut off from his emotions to enjoy any element of romance. But when she asked him about them he simply replied, 'oh yeah, I thought they could make the flat smell nicer'. She debated probing further but decided to leave it. He seemed a little anxious and the girl assumed it was because of work.

As always, they cooked dinner together; sharing funny stories and sweet kisses as they passed one another to grab ingredients. He was now a lot more open with the girl about his work life than when had they first seeing each other. For one, she knew all his colleagues by their first names, their bad habits and what it was about them that rattled him. The girl had come to learn that his colleagues were scared of him, especially his assistant, and that he wanted free of this world where he was constantly unhappy. He no longer liked his job and was looking for his next challenge. He was thinking that it just might be in New York. The idea half scared the girl – to think of life without him brought about a certain sadness, but it also half made her heart fill with joy, as she could very much picture him happy in NYC.

"I think we did an excellent job," the Shark told the girl, as they ate their delicious tortei da patate completely surrounded by candles.

"We certainly did, these taste great."

"I shouldn't have forgotten the cheese though," the Shark said for the fifth time that evening.

"Can you stop blaming yourself? We will make sure not to forget the cheese next time."

"Next time, yes. So...Skye," he paused, swallowing nervously. The girl watched the Shark play with his fork, his eyes fixed on his empty plate. He wasn't usually nervous. He almost looked vulnerable, and the idea tickled the girl.

Him? Vulnerable? Anxious? He is the most confident

person I know, she thought to herself.
The girl continued to study him curiously as she chewed.
"So...Skye. I'm not seeing anyone else."
The girl froze, mid-chew. Her stomach did somersaults. These were the words she had been dying to hear for the past five months. But she hadn't said anything, hadn't asked – things were going so well, they had become a team so quickly, so easily, and she had been terrified of ruining that. Plus, she was a firm believer that when a man is truly interested in a girl he simply does not see anyone else. Because he has no need to.
Unless he's a sex-obsessed looney. But that's a separate matter...
"...interesting," the girl managed to reply. *Interesting?! Is that all you can say?! You're an idiot, Skye.*
"Yes, I mean, I like seeing you. And I spend most of my time with you – and when I'm not with you I'm working. And working takes up a lot of my time, so even if I wanted to I couldn't..." he forced a laugh and the girl smiled, not sure what she could say to that. The idea of him kissing another girl, having sex with another girl, made both her blood boil and her stomach sink in pure heartbreak. "Sex is not something I need – if I wanted to fuck, I could fuck a... a...keyhole! So to speak. It's good company that means more to me, I realise this now."
He was trembling, and more than anything the girl wanted to get up and hug him, she really did. But she knew he wasn't a big hugger. He still didn't spoon her at night, or hug her in the mornings, the total opposite of all the men she had dated previously. It had taken some time to discipline herself to respect his ways of being. But sometimes, like in that moment, it was brutally hard.
He cleared his throat, collecting his finished plate and cutlery. "Anyway, just wanted to make that clear." His chair screeched painfully loud as he pushed it back and got up, walking over to the sink. She listened to the clinking of plates, as he subtly sighed in relief at the fact that the girl no longer could see his face. She looked around at the candles illuminating his kitchen. This had all been planned. The girl inwardly smiled.

He's worried he's going to lose me.
I mean something to him.
Even if it's little.
It's there.
It's there!
He cares.
You are not imagining it, Skye.

She finished her plate and got up, walking over to him. "Hey..."

He turned around to face the girl, still as anxious as before.

"We can wash the plates later. Let's go upstairs."

He nodded, wiping his hands with the kitchen towel.

"By the way, I'm not seeing anyone else either," the girl told him. His face relaxed, and he smiled ever so slightly, holding back as if afraid to reveal any sort of reaction to her statement.

"...interesting," he replied, half mocking her, and she grinned. He pulled the girl to him and kissed her sweetly. They looked at one another with smiles for a few seconds, before making their way upstairs.

"Breaking Bad?"

"Season 2."

Drop the Tude

"I can't believe they didn't take me. It's so unfair," the girl told him, as she pulled the onions out of the cupboard.

"Hmm," he replied, as he chopped the garlic.

"I mean, what did I expect? This industry only takes who they know."

"Hmm."

"Are you listening? Hey?"

He dropped his knife abruptly and turned to the girl. "Yes Skye, I'm listening. I've been listening since the day we met. And I've been waiting for you to evolve, grow in the way you approach your goals, but it seems your attitude is forever staying the same."

"What are you talking about?"

"You know what drew me to you, Skye? It wasn't your sexy dress or your heels; it was your strength. Fuck, you have a lot of strength and a lot of ambition. When we met you were blocking out that ambition due to fear, fear of failure, after what happened in the music industry, and I found this ridiculous – there is no one I believe can succeed more than the person standing in front of me now.

But then you started channelling it, and that was great to see. This is only the beginning for you, you're going to grow and become bigger and tougher and just...it's going to be amazing. And it's amazing for me to watch.

And when you started channelling your ambition, I started thinking: yes, now she's also going to re-evaluate her take on life, her way of getting things done. She's going to see that her current attitude doesn't work, that's not how people win.

Yet you're still complaining about the same things going wrong that you were a month ago, two months ago. You're not seeing that it's not about people choosing the ones they know Skye, it's about you going out there and getting what you fucking want. Finding a way to get it. One method doesn't work, you try another. And you keep trying. Why am I successful?

Because I never fucking gave up. And I am waiting for you to understand this, because if you don't take this on board you're never going to succeed."

Birthday

When the girl walked back up the marble stairs to the ground floor of the ridiculously expensive Primrose Hill restaurant, their table was empty. Confused, the girl glanced through the window to see the Shark smoking a cigarette on the pavement outside. He was looking into the distance pensively, as he breathed out smoke. She smiled, her heels click-clacking with every step as she made her way outside.

The air was surprisingly warm that night for London, even if it was June. The girl glanced at the time on her watch – 11:35PM.

"There's still 25 minutes left of your birthday," she told him, breaking him out of his daydream. He looked up and smiled at her, as if the sight of her approaching warmed him. "What would you like to do?"

"I thought we could go home, watch an episode of Suits, have a Whiskey…"

The girl smiled, but then remembered something.

"Hey, did you pay the bill?"

"Yes I did, whilst you were in the bathroom."

"No way! It's *your* birthday!" the girl reached for her purse, but the Shark put a hand on her arm.

"Please, Skye. You've done enough today. Let me pay for dinner." They stared at one another. With the Shark's hand on her arm, the girl realised this was the most contact they had had for a few hours. They had sat opposite one another at dinner, sharing stories and making plans for the summer. The girl had arrived at his place armed with gifts and a Breaking Bad cake she had got designed especially for him. The look on his face as he had opened that cake box had warmed her heart. "You're incredible Skye," he suddenly told her. They both leaned in and kissed – a quick peck. Another peck. A full on kiss. They let go, and smiled at one another.

The girl shivered, but she wasn't cold. *What the hell is going on?* She asked herself. There was something about that night. About getting him that cake. About everything that was happening. She thought about the man he had been on their first date – his one pillow on the bed, his working every weekend. Now he half worked and half spent it with the girl. He used to go running alone, but now they had their own joint running routine. Life was changing and fast.

When they went home that night, they talked and ate cake in bed and fell asleep watching a film. This, for the girl, was her new happy place. Or at least, one of them. It occurred to her that all her happy places now included the Shark.

That night, once they had fallen asleep after a glass of whiskey, the girl suddenly awoke in the middle of the night. The Shark was tossing and turning beside her, when he usually slept very still.

The girl suddenly felt an arm slip around her waist from behind her, and his breath on the back of her neck.

Her heart began racing, wondering if she was dreaming. She had never felt his breath on her neck before. She had never felt his arm around her – it was even more glorious than she had imagined. The moment was the most intimate she had ever felt in her entire life.

He's spooning me. The girl's eyes widened, not sure what to do. She only knew she had waited more than half a year to have his arms around her, to arrive at the moment where he *wanted* to have his arms around her.

Because the girl had realised that he had probably never felt a want to have his arm around any woman.

She had reached a new level of him. He was testing his limits. He was letting down his guard. He was there, in the moment with her. Not a thousand miles away.

She instantly turned around, and with half-closed, sleepy eyes, he lifted his arm. As casually as possible, as if it weren't a big deal at all, as if she hadn't wanted this from their very first date, she lay her head on his chest. He put his arm around her, tightly, holding her close, holding her as if he were afraid to lose her.

If that weren't enough, he then affectionately kissed her on the forehead, before resting his chin on top of her head.

What the hell is happening?

Has someone else taken over his body?
Is this really him?
Is he really cuddling me right now?
The girl in that moment knew that nothing had ever felt quite like home as the Shark's arms around her. Her heart was cartwheeling with emotions, and a part of her wanted to cry in sheer sadness at the fact that this moment could never be surpassed. Because she knew that nothing in life could ever surpass the beauty of this moment. She knew it. This moment was undefeatable.

I don't know what's happening right now, the girl thought to herself, *I really don't.*
Slow down.
Slow down!
But
I'm so happy.

We do not love halfway: We give everything or we give nothing. This is the human condition.

"So...I think I want to be a writer," the girl blurted out one night on a video call with the Shark from his hotel room in Prague.

His smile beamed back at her, both proud and excited for the girl.

"Finally! It's about fucking time! Yes Skye, yes! You have always been a writer, by the way. You've just been too scared to pursue it. Let's do this."

"'Let's do this'?"

"Well, I am the one that got rid of your writers' block, am I not? I want a 50% cut of your future earnings. We can buy a massive villa in Hawaii."

"You're such an asshole."

The Shark laughed, but his expression suddenly turned serious.

"You're a writer, Skye. This is your passion, this is who you are. Stay focused. You are more than capable of doing this."

Shut up, Heart

The girl arrived at the Shark's workplace soaked from the typical British weather, due to her idiotic decision to not bring an umbrella with her that day. She took the lift up to the 25th floor, trying to sort out her scruffy, wet hair in the lift mirrors and failing miserably.

Arriving at his office, she noticed through the glass windows that his assistant was crying. The girl froze, her hand on the doorknob, and her face looking in through the little door window.

Why the hell is she crying? He's always bloody making her cry, poor girl.

There were only a few people left in the Shark's office at that point, and she watched his assistant cover her face with her hands in despair.

"I can't do this! I give up!" bawled the 22-year-old small, Italian girl from behind her thick-framed glasses. The girl knew this was Ana, his assistant, because she had met her several times already. Not only that, but the Shark often spoke about work on their way home or at dinner; he loved to tell her stories from his day. She knew random facts about his colleagues, such as Ana was on a strict diet but kept stuffing chocolate into her mouth when she thought nobody was looking, and Brian, the assistant director, was having an affair with Mel from downstairs. The scandal! Whenever the girl visited the Shark's office, she felt as if she worked there too, only nobody else knew it.

He swung his chair around, his eyes widening at the sight of tears streaming down his assistant's face. He tried his best to appear unaffected, but the girl could see the panic in his eyes; it was the same kind of panic that appeared on his face whenever she tried to make him talk about his feelings.

"Hey, what's going on?" he got up, walking over to his assistant. He lifted a hand to place on her arm but hesitated, deciding instead to rest it on her desk. "Hey...it's okay to cry sometimes, you know. It's perfectly fine. I do it sometimes too," he paused, unaware that the girl was watching him through the window in fascination. "It's okay to cry. But give up? No, never. You don't ever give up. Otherwise, what the hell are you doing here?"

His assistant continued to cry even though she was trying her best to stop. The Shark took a deep breath in, choosing his next words carefully, and rubbing his forehead with his fingers like he always did when he was uncomfortable.

"You know, there's a fast food joint across the road from here, have you seen it?"

She nodded through tears.

"Right, have you seen one of the girls that work there? She's Spanish too, about your age. She might even be from Barcelona. She might share your name, she might even share your skills. But you know the difference between you two?"

Ana stared at the Shark, as if in a trance.

"She's working *towards* a dream, whereas you are *living* it. You are here, in this office, with this amazing opportunity, and with me helping you to better yourself. This is just the beginning, Ana! I see a lot of potential in you, I do. But, I need someone willing to work *insanely* hard to achieve results. That means working crazy hours and sometimes, that means getting things wrong. And that's okay, really, that's just part of life. But being able to try again and again until you get it right, *that* is the key here. Because this job is a bitch, believe me, I know, but it's also amazing. You need to be able to recognise where you are right now, the opportunity you have to become great at what you love. I'm looking for *that* individual.

I guess what I want to know is…are you that person, Ana? Are you going to be that person for me? Or do I need to pay a visit to that girl at the fast food joint?"

There was silence and his assistant wiped her tears and wailed enthusiastically, "no! I'm that person!"

"Good. Let's get back to it, then. Skye will be here soon."

The girl watched him walk back over to his chair as if recovering from battle.

She looked down at her chest. "Shut up," she whispered to her heart. "Shut up, you don't love him. You don't."

I don't believe that there is just one person in the universe for us, but I do believe that there are very few people in this world that can truly love us the way we truly love them.

I Bet You

The girl lay on the Shark's kitchen floor in fits of laughter as the man in front of her, dressed as Nick from Backstreet Boys, danced around to 'Everybody (Backstreet's Back)' that was blasting from his speakers. It was hard to think that it was less than a year ago that these two had had their first date. That on one side of the table had sat a very serious man, with very stern eyes, and whose goals had all been work-orientated. He had walked as if he had a stick stuck up his butt, and his jawline constantly tense. The girl, on the other hand, had been far too evasive of serious things, letting life pass her by without taking into consideration her future. Her favourite line had been '*tomorrow – I'll get it to it tomorrow*'.

Yet the girl lying on the floor of his kitchen laughing to the point that her stomach hurt, was in the midst of changing job, and had begun writing professional website bios as a side hobby. People were actually paying her to write! To do something she loved and had always loved. It was helping her develop various writing styles and she was enjoying putting effort into something she treasured.

The girl looked at the Shark in front of her, his eyes bright and ecstatic, as he danced around like an absolute twat to the boyband song. She was glad that she had been able to loosen him up a little, that he was now able to enjoy the little joys that life could bring. She could see it in his eyes that he was happier, and with this new found happiness he was able to accomplish even more in his work life. It was hard to think that this looney dancing horrendously bad in front of her had been leading a big meeting at work only hours earlier.

He wasn't losing his serious side, but gaining a fun one.

"Come on, you can't let me do this alone!" he shouted over the music, laughing, as he pulled her up from the floor. "Are you with me or not?!"

The Shark wasn't dancing around dressed as Nick Carter for no reason, by the way. The girl had made a bet that he couldn't go a week without eating a single chocolate biscuit; they were his kryptonite. Not being one to refuse a challenge, he had agreed to it with a confident smile, and had lasted an impressive five days, eleven hours, and thirty-five minutes.

The girl, who had never said no to dancing around to 90s boyband classics, was up like a shot.

"EVERYBODY! Rock your body!" she squealed, and he picked her up, putting her over his shoulders, as he hopped around the kitchen. She pulled off his blonde wig and put it on her own head, as they pretended to perform in front of an audience, when in reality their only spectators were the oven, the cooker, and the washing machine.

Once the song ended and he put her down, the girl noticed his flatmate, Tommaso, standing at the kitchen door, eating a salami sandwich.

"You two are a weird couple."

She made him more human, and in turn, he channelled her inner shark.

Red flags exist for a reason. Ignoring them will never, ever work in your favour.

Shark:

Listen Skye, I can't come to your party this weekend.
Sorry. Got a work dinner that night.
And Sunday I should work on a proposal.
See you soon though?
Will make it up to you. X

The Vanishing Act

The girl found 'Shark' in her contacts and pressed 'call'. It rang and rang and rang. This happened sometimes. He would disappear. He would act as if he didn't have a phone. He would stay at the office after hours and the girl would think he was with someone else. After all, they were not together, they had simply promised to not see anyone else. But that sort of promise can be broken in a heartbeat. Because he wasn't her boyfriend. Because he had made no *real* commitment to her.

She began crying, as she crawled onto her bed, burying her head under the pillow. The girl was so upset, so frustrated, when he did this. He was unreachable. And the girl felt as if she meant nothing to him. Like she could die whilst crossing the road and he wouldn't even care, wouldn't even know about it.

Her phone buzzed on the nightstand and she instantly picked it up.

```
                    Charles:
     He's here. He's not talking to me, in fact
     he called me a bunch of names. But he's here.
                   Don't worry.
```

His colleague, Charles, whom he worked on projects with, often text her to tell her where he was, to let her know he was alright. That he wasn't with someone else; he just simply didn't want to talk to her.

Attached to Charles' text was a picture of the Shark. He was at his desk, unaware that the picture was being taken. There was passive-aggression in his eyes as he worked on something on his laptop.

The Shark disappeared like this when things were going well between them, so damn well that he had to make sure he messed it all up. He would say something awful to upset her, something hurtful to push her away, to put her back at arm's length, and to remind her that she had no place in his world.

It worked, for the most part. Except once the girl was done crying into her pillow, he would come back. He would come back and he would convince her of how sorry he was, tell her that he had lost track of time, and that he was here now. He would tell the girl that she was overreacting, and act as if nothing had happened.

And she would let him.

This Night was Always Going to be Yours

The phone flashed and the girl picked up instantly. She didn't need to see what name was flashing on the screen to know it was him.

"What happened?!"

"Skye! I won! I won! I won!" his voice was happy, ecstatic, but shaky. For sure he was trembling. She could picture the Shark on the other side of the call, prancing around in the lobby of the chic building where they held the awards ceremony. His shirt sleeves rolled up, his forehead sweaty, and his free hand on his temple.

A wave of emotion came over the girl and she covered her mouth in shock.

"Oh my God!"

"I won! Skye, I'm coming home, I'm just getting a taxi, I'm coming straight home to you. You're still at mine, right?"

"Yes!"

"Stay right there! Don't move! Don't move, okay?"

"I'm not going anywhere, I'm here."

"Okay. Okay, I'll be right there!"

"Okay."

"Skye," the Shark said the girl's name the same way he always did – with a mix of urgency and love.

"Yes, baby?"

"I'm really glad to be able to share this moment with you. I can't believe…" his voice trailed off and there was silence.

"You were always going to win tonight. Remember this. You worked your ass off to get here. This was always yours, this night was always going to be yours."

"And I know exactly who I want to spend it with."

The girl smiled, even though he couldn't see her.

"You always believe in me, you're incredible."

"What's there to believe in? Belief in something that is real is not belief at all – it's just fact. You deserve this. You worked for this. And this is just the beginning. Now get here so we can celebrate."

"You know where I keep that special bottle of Whiskey, right?"
"Right."
"I'll get the chocolate biscuits. Breaking Bad?"
"Season 3? The episode where what's-his-name dies?"
"See you in 40-45 minutes."

"You know," the Shark would always begin, *"when I was a teenager, I wasn't spending my Saturday nights drinking and trying to find my next conquest. My friends did, but I didn't. I spent my Saturday nights working – on myself, on my skills, on my weaknesses.*

I was obsessed, and I still am. Because to become good at something, and I mean really fucking good, takes practise, effort, and dedication.

Life is made up of choices. You chose to spend your Saturday nights partying, I chose to gain from mine. And now look at us. I have a job I love, an incredible girl by my side, and I still am fucking obsessed with what I do. With bettering myself. Every. Single. Fucking. Day.

You, on the other hand, spend your days trying to steal my job.

So tell me, why are you still asking yourself the reasons I'm better than you?"

3AM

The girl awoke suddenly in the dead of night. This was strange for her – she usually slept straight through until morning. But when she awoke, she immediately noticed that the other side of the bed was empty. Bewildered, she gave it a few minutes – perhaps the Shark was in the bathroom. But when he did not come back into the bedroom and there was total silence in the flat, she began to worry.

She got up, shivering, but decided to leave everything to go find him. She was too infested with worry to think of such trivial things such as grabbing a jumper on the way. She stepped out and checked the bathroom; it was empty. And so she made her way to the kitchen, beginning to tremble now. The entire flat was dark and she walked barefoot onto the cold, tiled floor of the kitchen.

In the distance she spotted him. He sat on the floor with his knees up to his face, crying into them. The girl could not believe what she was seeing. This was not the person that had kicked everyone's butts at a big meeting at work only hours earlier. This was not the person that constantly made his assistant cry. This was not the person that at dinner had been laughing and joking with the girl, tickling her before they fell asleep.

She suddenly recalled him withdrawing pretty quickly and moving to his side of the bed; he had not even said goodnight. But the girl had thought nothing of it and assumed he had simply fallen asleep before he could remember to do so.

There had been no signs of pain, turmoil, or agony in him. None more than usual, anyway. Yet this was what the girl saw in front of her now.

She ran over, but he did not look up, he just continued sobbing to himself, his head between his legs. The girl was in pieces – to see the person she loved in so much pain and not knowing why it was happening. Guilt consumed her, realising that she hadn't been able to predict it. And she cursed herself for not being able to see it coming.

"What is it? Tell me, hey...tell me!" the girl tried to yank his arm away so that she could see his face, but he was too strong for her. "Tell me!" she demanded. It hurt too much to see him like this; she needed to help him. She was sobbing too at this point – she couldn't take it anymore; her heart was aching at what she saw in front of her.

He finally raised his head slightly. His cheeks were shiny with tears, his eyes filled with pain, and the girl, for the first time, saw the full extent of his tortured soul.

"What happened?" she asked softly, reaching out a hand to caress his cheek, but he simply backed his head away.

"Nothing-"

"Fuck you! Something is wrong. What is it?"

"It's an off day, Skye. That's all. Not everything is going my way. It gets overwhelming."

The girl studied his face as he looked straight ahead. She sat down beside him, so that they were both looking at the oven across from them. There was silence in his flat; not a sound could be heard. All the girl could hear was a single line that kept repeating itself in her head – *I must get him out of the black hole.*

"You once told me in the beginning that me and you have some sort of crazy connection. That we could be sitting in front of a wall and you could find infinite things to talk about. Because you somehow trust me. And we somehow bring everything to life. Well, here we are," she pointed to the oven with her thumb. "It's as good as a wall."

The girl slowly reached out to caress his cheek, and this time he didn't move.

I must get him out of the black hole.

He sighed, and by this point he had stopped crying. "There's too much going at the same time. Everyone is always expecting me to be this tough Shark; always mean, always the motherfucker you don't wanna mess with. But I have pain myself. I have pain Skye, from the past, from the present, I just don't have time to process from the struggle. I can't...I can't...I just need to break down sometimes, it's natural, no? I need that right now. I'll be fine. I'll be fine Skye, you should go to bed-"

"No. I'm staying."

The Shark closed his eyes, as the girl continued to caress his cheek. Tears trickled down his cheek and the girl gulped, trying to refrain from grabbing him and holding him in her arms. He needed to talk. He had to share. There was no going back from this.

I must get him out of the black hole.

"I'm always expected to be this tough person, I'm not always tough, Skye. I'm not always tough."

"I know, baby," she ran a hand through his hair, affectionately. "I know. And you don't have to be."

"But that's the thing, I feel like I always have to be. Like I'm constantly proving people wrong. I can't stop."

"Proving what wrong and to who?"

"I was a loser at school, Skye. I was a loser. I couldn't even stand up for myself. I was getting beaten up every day other school. And my father kept telling me I wasn't a man, that I needed to become a man and face things."

The girl studied him in fascination as she continued to caress his cheek. "That's why you're not afraid of anything anymore."

"Of course I am, Skye. I'm still human. I'm still afraid of lots of things. But yes, I've become a lot tougher, and cold. I'm so cold, Skye. You don't know how many girls I've made cry in my life."

The girl thought of his self-destructive personality and how many times she had cried herself to sleep after something he had said or done to hurt her. But she was still there; she loved this warm side to him, she was pulled in by it.

"When I turned 18 I swore I'd prove everyone wrong. Everyone that bullied me, that called me a loser. And I did. And the satisfaction I get from it, Skye...you can't imagine. It's better than sex."

"You can't live your life trying to prove everyone wrong – you should be doing it for yourself," she told him.

"But that's the thing – I *do* do it for the satisfaction of proving other people wrong. It's the only way I *can* do it, it's the only way I can get up in the morning – by being successful, by being what nobody thought I could be. I'm doing it, Skye! I'm doing it!"

The girl studied his sad eyes, and realised the Shark had more problems than she had first anticipated. She had known he had pain to deal with, that he struggled with human emotions slightly more than the average person, but this was a completely different level of agony. And he had built it up over the years with no release. It just festered inside of him, hidden behind the mask of this tough, no-bullshit Shark.

"Skye, you should go to bed."

"No," she said, firmly.

"Skye-"

"I'm staying."

He gave up, sighing, and raised his arm so that the girl could rest her head on his chest. She did so, and there they sat on the Shark's kitchen floor, cuddling. They hadn't cuddled since his birthday. He hadn't tried to spoon her again and the girl hadn't asked to feel his breath on the back of her neck again, no matter how much she craved it. It had to be him who wanted it, not she who requested it. This was a rule the girl lived by.

His arm around her now, she realised she never wanted to leave. It was there again – that feeling of being home. It was so powerful, so demanding, the girl felt afraid of what she might say or what she might feel when he had his arm around her like he did just then.

"We're going to stay here all night if we have to," she told him. The girl was cold, freezing in fact, but she didn't dare leave the Shark's side for a second. Not even to go get the duvet. She was afraid to leave him with his pain, his fears, his doubts. And she was afraid to leave his arms and this feeling of home. It was imperative that she stayed put on his chest, feeling his skin against hers.

It was imperative.

I must get him out of the black hole.

The girl often got asked what she thought love was. She found the question outrageous every time she was asked. How was she supposed to know? Did she look like an expert?! As a kid reading Great Expectations she had related more to Miss Havisham than she ever did to Pip; that should tell you everything you need to know.

But on days that the girl was brave enough to be honest with herself and someone asked her what she thought love was, she didn't think of Romeo and Juliet. She didn't think of roses and chocolates, a good date she had been on or the perfect first kiss. She didn't think of I love you's or sweet words exchanged on social media that she would then screenshot to her friends. None of that was love, to the girl.

What she did think of was 6AM runs with the Shark. The sound of their ridiculously expensive running shoes jogging in sync through Holland Park. She thought of how they would always stop at the same time but never the same location. And that this was done with no exchange of words. Not because they were out of breath or because they had a particular need to be quiet, it was just that the other's company was enough. Nothing needed to be said, the silence would speak for them. And that, for the girl, was love. Or at least, her perception of love.

The Break Up

Why hadn't she listened? Why had she thought she could make a difference? She should have known better. She should have understood that it didn't matter if he kissed her sweetly on the forehead at night, or if they went on Sunday morning runs together. It didn't matter if he had learnt how to share his life with someone else, little by little. That he was now more considerate, more caring, and a warmer person. None of that mattered. Even if it was important to both of them. Even if it meant something to both of them. And it didn't matter because he had issues that she couldn't even begin to understand.

His compulsion to self-destruct was toxic; he had a constant need to obliterate any happiness in his life. And what the girl had to understand was that it was not something she could stop or prevent. By loving him and caring for him, she couldn't prevent his darkness from coming out. It was there – it lived inside of him, festering inside his soul.

But, like most people in love, she refused to believe this, to accept this. She didn't want to acknowledge that there were two separate sides to him. That he could not live one without the other. That if she wanted his good side, she had to take his bad side with it.

Yet the question was not: does she want this? The question was and had always been:

Can she survive this?

The Request

It was one grey autumn afternoon that the Shark stood in the middle of his flat, asking the girl to share something with him. Anything. You see, it wasn't just the Shark that had problems - the girl seemed to have major issues with intimacy too, just a different type. She found it incredibly hard to share anything personal about her life with anyone. But she had assumed that since falling in love was something new to her, that it would be different with him. Yet it wasn't. Sharing still seemed like weakness to the girl; a weakness she wasn't able to give into.

"Being together means sharing, Skye. I'm here waiting for you to share with me, I'm always waiting," the Shark told her, in a shaky voice. The girl's silence told the Shark his answer; abstaining from speech was always her response when put in this situation. When being asked something of her. But this time he pulled her gently by the hand out of his bedroom and into the kitchen. He pointed to a spot on the floor.

"You remember what happened here? When I was crying in the middle of the night on this floor and you came and you held me? I had never let anyone see that side to me, not even my own mother."

The girl remained mute, and fought hard against tears of frustration. She was angry with herself, with her inability to open up. She didn't understand it, why she was this way.

"I want to be there for you the way you are there for me. You've entered my world now Skye; nobody has been here before. Let me be that person for you."

The girl didn't know what self-destruction truly was until she met him. Until she saw his necessity to destroy himself again and again, to kill anything that could make him happy, to obliterate any possibility of fulfilment in his personal life.

And he would destroy these things to make sure that they could never come back, that they could never again spawn any glimmer of joy that could reach his heart, that could remind him that he had one. Because he did, under all those layers of arrogance and self-righteousness he did have a heart, and a marginally big one too. But he didn't like to acknowledge this fact, with himself or with anyone else. He was convinced the entire world was the enemy, when in reality his biggest enemy was himself.

The Cake

The girl lay on the Shark's lap, as he combed her hair affectionately with his fingers. She was in her dark place, and when the girl was in her dark place, nobody could save her.

The XX played softly in the background, and she cherished these sweeter moments even more so now that they were fighting a lot.

"You have no idea who I am or what kind of person I can be," the girl told him, as darkness possessed her. When this happened she placed blame on herself for everything bad in her life, and she let the guilt consume her.

But she was lonely there and trying to aggravate the Shark to make him revert to his dark side too, to join her, so that they could be dark together. But he had refused. And he had refused so well.

"Yes I do," the Shark replied, calmly.

"No you don't, stop pretending you know me. I don't share anything with you, you're on the other side of this wall."

The Shark fidgeted in his chair as she said that, but continued combing through the girl's hair. He was hurt by her words but was adamant not to let it show, because he knew this was what she wanted. This was what her dark side always wanted.

"You know what Skye, you're right. There are so many things I still don't know about you, because you choose to keep them to yourself. And I'm here waiting for you to take that step, I would love more than anything for you to share more with me," he paused, thinking carefully about his next words.

"But... you know, I remember this girl...this amazing girl that got me a cake for my birthday. Nobody has ever in their life got me a cake for my birthday. My mother would make me a small pie or something, but that was it. Nobody had ever done anything like that for me, nobody had ever made me feel special on my birthday or that I'm worth being made special for. You came along and you brightened everything up. You accept me for the cold bastard that I am, and to do that can't be easy, I know I'm difficult, and it takes a certain warmth to do what you've done, to change what you've changed about me. So whatever you think about yourself, and some of it may be true, there's an extraordinary warmth to you that defeats all the bad, trust me. It's a wonderful warmth."

Secret tears streamed down the girl's cheek as he continued to comb through her hair, lovingly. She wished she could stop time forever. To when the Shark was caring, to when he looked after her, to when he loved her.

To when the girl *knew* he loved her.

"I'm fucked up, Skye! I'm fucked up! Why would you want to be with someone fucked up?! All I will do is hurt you! I will hurt you, and I won't even be sorry! I won't! Because I care about nobody but myself, Skye! You should know this already, you know me better than I do! I can't give you anything, and we are both free to see who we want! We never committed ourselves to each other! We are just passing time! Don't get attached to me! How many times have I told you?!"

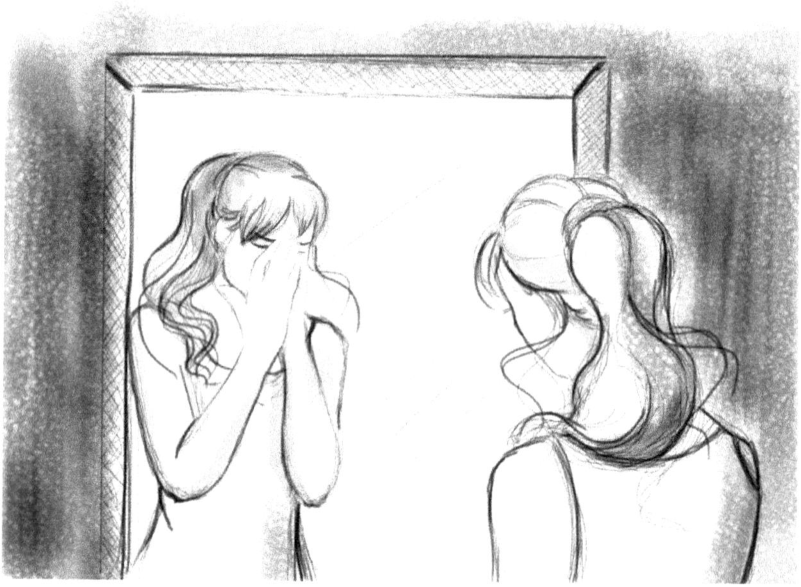

"I always disappear, it's what I do. But with you I can't. I can't, Skye. My mum would never believe me if I told her what I was doing right now – begging you to stay, to stay in my life, talking about my feelings... This is hard for me, Skye. This is damn hard, I've never done it before, I've never done it for anyone."

The Limit

The girl lay on the Shark's bedroom floor in fits of tears. She was in pieces, and she knew her heart was broken. She had never had it broken before and so had no previous experience to compare it to, but she knew it was broken. Something felt different. She felt a shift. And she knew this was her limit. There was no going back this time.

Never had she felt so weak, so shattered by another person. Her pain in that moment was a direct result of the words that had come out of the Shark's mouth. That ache in her stomach, that agony, it was a direct result of the person she loved.

The things he had said to her had been so ruthless, so cutthroat, that she wouldn't have wished them upon her worst enemy.

He has destroyed me. He is a monster.

These were the words running through the girl's head as she lay there. He had collected her weaknesses over time and used them against her when he needed to, when he was at his most defensive.

Why?

To win.

To feel superior over her.

But this was the girl's limit. All the happy moments shared were now obsolete. All she saw was a monster. A troubled, messed up monster, and she wanted nothing more to do with him.

She didn't understand it, how someone could destroy another person so easily and not feel anything. He was showing no remorse. He had enjoyed it.

She knew then that she should have listened when her gut had told her to stay away.

She knew then that she had to walk away this time.

"Get out of my life!" The girl screamed in despair. "Get the fuck out of my life and stay out!"

"Skye-"

The girl picked up one of his books and threw it across the room. "Are you listening to me?! You're too fucked up! You're a misogynistic, arrogant, toxic-"

"Skye! I can't leave, I can't let this go-"

"GET THE FUCK OUT OF MY LIFE! GET OUT! GET OUT! GET OUT!" the girl screamed at the top of her lungs. Her voice died down, as she broke into tears. "Get out of my life, please. Please, just get out," she begged, softly.

Shark:

Skye, please answer.
Come on, Skye.
I know you're reading my messages.
Don't be like this.
Please.

The Step

The girl stood outside the job agency, anxiously peering into their busy offices. Women in pencil skirts were running around dealing with several clients at once.

"You have to press the buzzer," said a woman who appeared next to her.

"Oh." Before the girl could move, the stranger had pressed it for her and strolled into the offices as if she knew the place inside out. One of the women in pencil skirts suddenly marched over to the girl with a big smile on her face.

"Hello, can I help you?"

What do I say? I've never been to a job agency before. Do I just tell her what I'm here for?

"Yes, I'm…I'm looking for a new job."

"Well you've come to the right place! Where do you currently work?"

"Oh, up the road, at a recruitment agency…in fact I've ducked out on my lunch break…"

"Oh well that's alright, we'll have you back there before your lunch hour ends. What type of job are you looking for?"

"Um…" *Good question. Why didn't I think of this before I came here? Stupid, stupid Skye.* "What do you have?"

"Administrative, secretarial, legal…"

"Legal?" *Like Suits. You could be like Harvey Spectre.*

"Yes, dear. At law firms, courthouses…"

"Legal jobs – I want to apply for legal jobs," the girl decided, there and then.

"Wonderful. Follow me over to my desk, sorry, what's your name?"

"Skye," she told her, as she sat herself down in front of the woman's desk.

"Nice name! Do you have a copy of your CV, Skye?"

"Yes," the girl got it out and handed it to her. She watched as she scanned through it, licking her thumb as she flipped to the second page. When her eyes looked up to meet the girl's, she found the stranger impossible to read.

She has essentially just read my life story so far, and she has no reaction. That can't be good.

"You've worked in music a lot," she told the girl, as if awaiting confirmation.

"Yes."

"Why did you leave that to work in recruitment?"

"Took a break."

"Well the admin side to your current job should help you get interviews for legal jobs, but we might need to get rid of the music business experience as it is irrelevant in this industry. Is that OK?"

"Sure," the girl told the woman, trying her best to hide the fact that she felt something hit her hard in the stomach. "Let's wipe it all out, no problem."

How many times a day I looked
At my phone
Waiting for his name
To pop up on the screen
How much my heart jumped out
Of my chest
Every time I saw that name
And heard that glorious sound
My phone would make.
How I leapt up to read it
To pretend I wanted nothing more
To do with him
When it wasn't true
I loved him
And I loved seeing his name
Pop up
Over and over and over again

Black Olives

"Come with me to Italy for Christmas."

The girl suddenly dropped the kitchen knife and it nearly landed on her foot, but she moved away in time. She looked up at the Shark, her cheeks burning.

Is he MAD? Why is he like this?

They hadn't seen each other in two months, when the girl had told him to never contact her ever again. She had had enough, his dark side was tearing her apart. And so she had made the decision to opt out of this emotional mess. To choose herself. To fall out of love and move on.

And yet there she was, in his kitchen, a mere eight weeks later. And as cliché and pathetic as it seemed to the girl, they appeared to be drawn to one another.

He was cooking the girl dinner, one of his famous homemade pizzas that she had had dreams about since they had been apart.

"Italy? You want me to go to Italy with you? For Christmas?"

The Shark had asked the girl what she was doing over Christmas and she had simply replied that she was spending it with her family. When she had turned the question around on him, she had anticipated being told he was going back to Italy to do the same, but the last thing she had expected was an invitation to go with him.

"Yes, come with me. Spend a few days with me. We can talk, I have things to tell you, I can show you my hometown..."

But the girl had already grabbed her handbag and was heading for the door. This was a no-go zone for her. She couldn't go back. She had been promised a talk, nothing else. Not an invitation to fly to another country to play happy families.

"Skye, hold on, hold on..."

"You're insane. Two months ago I told you to leave me alone-"

"Then why are you here? You could have said no, you could have blocked me, but you didn't. Because we are both here for the same reason, feeling the same things the other is," the Shark told the girl. "Now, I'm an asshole and I know this, you know this too; there's parts to that that I guess will never change. I know I hurt you, but there are things that *have* changed about me, and I only realised this when you sent me that final message.

At first I thought you were right: We can't continue like this. So as amazing as it was to spend that time together, it must end, like it always does. I can't stay with anyone and that's fine, you know my issues with that. But then something different happened the next day, something that has never happened before: I was sad. I was really sad, Skye. And as time went on it only got worse, I only missed you more, I only thought about you more, until one day I realised...something is missing.

There's something missing in my life, Skye. I can feel it. Something has changed, and it happened when we started seeing each other. Something good, something that made me wake up on in the morning with a smile on my face. It's not about having 'someone', I've never cared about having 'someone' and you know this - it's about having *you*. What we had was real, Goddamn it. It was real. Every day when I have my meetings and I have to use 'our' word with clients, the word that made us laugh for an entire *day*, I think of you. Of us laughing our heads off at it until our stomachs hurt. That for me is my happy place.

You know how many times a day I have to use that word? A zillion, Skye. And every time I use it I think of you, every damn time. I'm always thinking of you, Skye. I wonder how you are, what you're doing. And I'm not ready to let you go. No. I refuse to, I'm sorry. I want to work on it, on us, I want to fix this. And it all starts with a dinner. So now it's up to you. Do you want to grab the black olives for me, or head for the door?"

Shark:

Since we're both looking for new places to live, why don't we live together?

Skye:

Are you mad?! And why are you texting me this? You could have brought it up tonight at dinner! You crazy shark!x

Shark:

Well I'm not canned tuna, am I?x

Skye:

You most definitely are not.

Shark:

See you tonight.
P.S. I think we could really do it.x

"I need you in my life. You have become a part of my life, don't you see that? And don't tell me this is because of sex – I didn't touch you last time you were here, I didn't fucking touch you, remember? You know how hard that was for me? I'm a fucking animal and you know this, but I didn't fucking touch you, because... because laughing with you is better than sex, Skye. It's better. What we have is real, it's reached a part of me I never thought possible. You know why I came back? Because I couldn't go on suffering anymore, it was too much. I came back because I can't let you go. I need you in my life, please don't close this door without thinking properly. You know you're impulsive, Skye. Don't be impulsive, please think this through."

New Year's Eve

It's 3AM on New Year's Eve and the girl is tipsy in a dark corner of some bar near the Tower of London. Her friend is too drunk to realise she is no longer dancing with her, and that she has actually slipped off the dance floor to check her messages. There, on her screen, were messages from the Shark. She had blocked him on all technology only the day before, and unblocked him within several hours. She couldn't do it. She couldn't block him out of her life like that. It wasn't that simple. As soon as she had unblocked him they had chatted for a while, as if nothing had happened. As if they were okay, as if they had always been okay.

The girl clicked on the video he had just sent her of the club he was at, and some voice clips she couldn't hear over the shitty music playing at the bar. Blame it on the alcohol, or blame it on the fact that she was undoubtedly in love with the asshole on the other side of the conversation, but she couldn't help typing what was going on in her head.

Skye:

I have to tell you something!

Shark:

Ok… what is it?

Skye:

You're special to me. But it's a secret, sssssh. Don't tell anyone.

Pause.
Nothing.

The girl stared. And stared. And stared.

Shark:

You're special to me too, Skye. You have no idea just how much.

The Shark and the girl were in two different cities, in two different countries, celebrating the same thing. They had broken up, for the final time – he had hurt her again and now she knew she couldn't be with him anymore. They were supposed to have set off on their own separate paths by now, so why hadn't they? Why were they instead texting each other on New Year's Eve from dark corners of bars, whilst their friends had a good time? Why was the girl telling him he was special to her? And just how did she know that he was staring at his phone screen with a smile as he read that message?

The girl had been told time and time again that he was bad news, that he would always be too scared to let the walls down and too stubborn to change. Theoretically, they had no chance. They were destroying each other, and the girl knew it. She knew it and by then she also knew that they could no longer go on like this, that one day she would have to find the courage to block him, to push him out of her life for good. But that connection between them, a connection so strong that it could be felt even when they were a hundreds of miles apart, was something the girl had never felt before. Never had such a feeling made her feel more alive. And she wouldn't swap it for anything - all the boring dates, empty conversations, meaningless kisses – these things only ever stole moments from her, not feelings. None of it had ever held a candle to their conversations, their kisses, and the way he could make her laugh until her stomach hurt.

In that moment, the girl decided rather than to dwell on what was to come, she would instead take in the good. Because it was a pure kind of good – this connection they had. And she promised herself that night to preserve it, to keep it with her, no matter how dark the tunnel got.

The Tie

"Skye, I need you in my life. I need you, Goddammit. And I have never needed anyone. I'm a fucking animal. I'm a lone wolf. But somehow, and I still don't understand how it happened but – you're a part of my life. You've become a part of my life."

"*Stop!* Stop coming back, stop hurting me like this-"

"Skye, I'm not trying to hurt you, not anymore. I just...I...I don't like doing my tie in the mornings."

"*What?!*"

"Everyday for the past ten years, I have done my tie by myself in the mirror. And I have been content doing it, beyond content. But then this girl, this amazing girl who pushed me and inspired me and handled me at my worst, she began doing it for me. And when she would do it she would look me in the eye with love, with compassion, as if I were special to her, as if I were different from everyone else, and I would think, does this incredible girl, this girl who both looks after me and is not afraid to be straight with me, does she really think I'm special? And not because of my job or my achievements, but because of who I am? Nobody has ever looked at me like that."

The girl caressed his cheek, affectionately. "You *are* special, never forget this."

"Skye, I don't want anyone else to do my tie in the mornings. It has to be you. I refuse to let it be anyone else."

The Words

"I'm back on Sunday, let's meet up and talk about this then," the Shark told the girl over video chat. The girl studied him as he sat nervously in his hotel room in Rome, loosening his tie having just come back from a big client meeting.

"I don't think so. I think we need that space right now."

"Space, Skye?! I'm in Italy, I think we're pretty far apart already!"

"I can't deal with your dark side anymore, I told you."

"I know, Skye. But that's why I want to talk face-to-face about this," the Shark told the girl with serious eyes.

"You always do this, you're brutal and then you switch back to your softer side, it's exhausting-"

"Skye, tell me you hate me, that I'm a fucking bastard, yell at me, but don't leave. I can't lose you. It's not an option."

The girl stared back at his solemn expression. He was close to tears. The hard, cold bastard was nowhere in sight. Staring back at her was a fragile man, a man she loved very much. So much so that the thought of him not being a part of her life actually physically hurt to think about. But she knew if she stayed she would only be exposing herself to more pain.

"We've talked about this. I told you-"

"I love you, Skye."

The girl froze in front of her laptop, not believing what she was hearing. After an entire year of wanting, wishing, imagining what it would like to hear those words come out of his mouth, there they were. As clear as day.

"I love you! Can't you see that? We can't end it like this. After everything. Skye…"

A part of her was angry, angry for his confession under such circumstances. Just when she was leaving, just when she was trying to separate herself from him. Was it even real, his words? Or was it simply said to make her try to stay? She didn't understand, she couldn't. She only knew she had to save herself. Nobody else was going to do it for her.

"I'm tired, I'm going to sleep."

"Skye-"
"Goodnight." As soon as she slammed the laptop shut, she remained perfectly still in the shock of what she had just heard. She played his words in her head, over and over and over...

The girl knew she had to let it go, she had known for a few weeks now. It was only going to end badly for her, and she had a chance to prevent it. But she had avoided the subject, the idea, of letting him go. Because in truth, no matter how good she was at giving other people advice, how sensible she was with her words, the truth was that at times she had the emotional strength of a flamingo. It was embarrassing.

She found it ruthlessly hard to let go of something special, for the simple reason that special things were a rare occurrence for her. She did not see sparkle and charm in every person she met, she did not develop feelings or an attachment to someone at the touch of a hand or at verbal promises.

It took much more for her to feel something, and it took much more for her to leave that something behind.

You Did It

When the Shark and the girl broke up for the final time, they tried, in vain, to remain friends. The Shark especially, had a hard time with the thought of losing the girl from his life forever. But it was insanely difficult for both of them, and though they text each other regularly and encouraged one another in work, they were both unhappy and they knew it. The girl smiled when she received good luck texts from the Shark before her job interviews, but would feel empty when she realised she would not be able to go over to his flat and tell him all about it over some wine and one of his delicious pizzas.

The Shark too, felt joy in being able to wish her luck before her interviews, but sadness at the awareness that that was all he would be able to do. There was a line between them now, and neither of them could cross it.

One day at work, the girl received a call from him. "Skye don't panic, okay? But are you able to come to the flat?"

He had hurt his back again, and was temporarily paralysed on his bedroom floor.

"WHAT?!" the girl raced over as fast as humanly possible. The idea of the Shark being in pain made her heart physically ache.

When she opened his bedroom door and walked in, she had to cover her mouth to stop herself from gasping.

"Fancy seeing you here," he said in a strained voice. The usually tough Shark was lying on the floor in his boxers, pale in the face and hands trembling. He looked like a vulnerable boy, and the girl could tell he was in extreme pain.

"Oh my God, I have to call an ambulance-"

"No, no, Skye. Remember what happened last time? No, we can fix this ourselves. Come here."

The girl slowly bent down in front of him, and he put a hand on her cheek.

"Focus, okay? I'm gonna be fine. You just need to help me get to the bed."

"No, no, no-"

"Yes, Skye. You can do this. You are the only one I trust. We can do this. Remember when you thought you couldn't change your life? And now look, you're changing it. You are the strongest person I know. I know you can do this," he paused, "heave me under the arms to get me onto the bed."

The girl got up, shaking, and did what he told her. He was heavier than expected, and as she carried him to the bed he kept saying, 'you're nearly there, keep going Skye'. Once she had successfully reached the bed, she gently dropped him onto his mattress and sighed in relief. She instantly lay her head on his chest and cried. He held her close.

"It's okay, you did it. You did it. I told you you could," the Shark kissed her hair. But the girl wasn't crying over his back. She was crying over the girly bracelets and earrings that were scattered all around his room.

The pain she felt in that moment was so horrendous, so unbearable, it was only then that she understood that letting him go could never be as painful as this. She knew in that moment that she would never return to this flat or cry in his arms ever again. That she would have to leave his key and everything else behind. She could not look after him anymore; she had to start looking after herself.

If it doesn't come from you, it will never stand.
If it doesn't come from you, it is validation from others that feeds you.
This is not strength, nor will it get you to strive for what you really want.

The First Day

The girl nervously pranced back and forth, as her eyes remained glued on the law firm across the street from her. To say she was anxious would be an understatement – she was trembling, and she hadn't even entered the building yet.

The girl peeled her eyes away from the humungous building to look down at what she was wearing – a ridiculously smart dress, with even smarter shoes – all insanely expensive of course, but you need to spend if you want results. And she wanted results.

What am I doing? The girl asked myself, as she bit her lip. *What the hell am I doing?*

She had left her old job in recruitment to work for a law firm.

She had left her *permanent* job in recruitment to temp at a law firm.

She had left her reliable, stable, dead-end job, to try and make something of herself.

The girl wanted to be a lawyer. She liked law, she had always liked law.

"Aren't you a writer?" her brother had asked.

"Yes, but I can't make money off of it, not now anyway – I need a career path."

So there she was, determined to be the real Harvey Spectre. She was still writing of course, but she was also reading lots of law books too, to prepare her for the role. The girl was to be a legal assistant, and had been very lucky to get this opportunity – they usually didn't take people that didn't have *some* sort of legal background.

I can do this.
I am bright and sharp and ready for this.

Just then, a sharply dressed man with a briefcase passed the girl and crossed the road. He turned around to look at her – she smiled, but his expression remained blunt, and he kept walking.

The girl quickly pulled out her phone.

Skye:

I can't do this!!!

Sofia:

Are you at work already? I miss you :(why did you leave me?

Because I didn't want to be stuck there forever.

Skye:

You'll be fine, Sofia!

I took a picture of the massive building, and sent it to her.

Sofia:

Oh wow! It didn't look that big on the website!

Skye:

That's what she said.

Sofia:

Hahaha. You will never change. Go knock them dead, Skye!

Sofia:

Ok.

    I put my phone away, took a deep breath in, and crossed the road.

New Stranger

The girl could just about make out the Greek's face in her dimly lit bedroom. She was naked and lying on top of him, talking bullshit about something or other. They were trying to pass the time in-between sex pretending they had some sort of connection other than a sexual one. Sex after the Shark was like a downgrade, no matter how good it was physically. It missed that something that only the Shark could bring to the table. Cuddles? The girl felt nothing. Kisses? The same. She had sex purely to satisfy her needs.

"Don't wear make-up, you look prettier without," the Greek suddenly interrupted her.

The girl froze, mid-sentence, having never been able to react well to a compliment. But she surprised herself by smiling coolly down at him. He was an insanely beautiful human being. He was a model/personal trainer, and when they were in each other's company she couldn't help but study every inch of his beautiful face.

"Are you trying to distract me from the fact that you want to order pizza?"

That's it Skye, don't blush. The girl feared that if she stopped to think about this Greek God considering her pretty, that her 16 year old self would most likely appear next to them doing cartwheels.

"I'm serious though, don't wear make-up; you're pretty enough to pull it off." Silence. "Right now you look....really good..." his voice died away and he kept his eyes fixed on her, curiously.

She stared down at his gorgeous face, finding it strange how she could find him so beautiful and yet not fascinating at all. She was sure it was the same for him.

What an odd symmetry we have, she thought.

"Okay," was the only thing she seemed able to reply, before changing the subject completely.

109

Superficial desires are the easiest to obtain, and because they are instantaneous, your want for them only grows the more you receive. This desire becomes a pattern, and your need for more, that greediness, only increases. Satisfaction doesn't exist when something is instantaneous.

Shark:

Skye, can I call you?
I want to talk to you about something.
Sorry to bother.
I know it's been 3 months.
But I hope you'll talk to me.

Curiosity Killed the Cat

It's been three months, the girl said to herself as she stared at his name flashing on her phone screen.

Before picking up she took a deep breath in, as if she were about to jump into the deep end of a pool. That's what it always felt like when she got involved with the Shark in any way, and part of the attraction was that mystery of the Unknown. She had no control over her feelings and neither did he. But as a kid she had always leapt straight into the deep end of any pool rather than the shallow; she never saw the point in jumping in where she knew her feet could touch the ground. Where was the fun in that?

The Shark and the girl spoke as if they had never cut ties, as if they had never ruined each other with some of the worst things you could possibly ever say to another person. They had learnt that night just how ridiculously talented they both were at hurting one another.

But that all seemed a blur now, taken over by the reminder that their history ran much deeper than that one incident.

At one point the Shark couldn't get his words out; he was stuttering, backing out of what he wanted to say. There was fear in his voice, she could detect it a mile away. The cocky and arrogant persona had melted away and he suddenly couldn't string a sentence together. She said his name and it triggered something, it demanded his full attention.

"Tell me?" he said, as if her saying his name had soothed him. As if he had wanted to hear her say his name since the day they had parted ways.

"Spit it out," she said in an authoritative tone, "what do you want to tell me?"

"I...I...just...I think I should call you back later, or tomorrow, I'll definitely call you back tomorrow..."

But the girl knew he wouldn't call back tomorrow. He would disappear for a couple more months until he would pluck up the courage to call her again. The girl didn't have any patience anymore for his games.

"Tell me right now or not at all."

This was the moment of truth, the moment she had been waiting for. Would he run away or be brave? Had he become fearless in their time away from one another?

"Okay Skye," he replied, and the girl was sure he was pacing the room on the other side of the line, pushing his hair back with his fingers like he always did when nervous. "Okay Skye, I'll tell you..." he took a deep breath in, and he had the girl on the edge of her seat. "I want you to come and work with me, the project is still new-"

A punch to the stomach for the girl, and anger took over immediately. "Why do you do this? Why do you come back every 3 months, do you have a timer on your phone? *Time to send Skye a message*'? Remind her of how much I can fuck with her head?"

"Working together doesn't mean it's going to be hurtful..."

"Anything with you is going to be hurtful. You bring pain. You're an emotional masochist. A misogynistic, egotistical-"

"I can see you're still angry at me-"

"I love you! Of course I'm angry at you!" the girl managed to blurt out. She was now trembling and finding it hard to keep the phone pressed to her ear. The silence between them seemed to last a lifetime.

"Skye..." the Shark finally said, "*do* you love me?"

"Yes." Another silence now, and tears rolled down her cheek. "Seriously though, do you ever stop to think about it? About why you keep pushing to have me in your life? Again and again you come back. It was *you* who was the asshole, it was *your* actions, *your* words, that made me cut you out. I've never been the girl to chase a guy, so your out was easy. Really easy. I let you go and I did not ever look back. So why do you keep coming back? Why go to the trouble of messaging me every few months?"

"Because I need to always know that you are okay. I need to always know it, Skye. You don't want me in your life, that's fine, but I need to always know that you're okay. I don't know why, okay? I just do."

"Goodbye," the girl hung up, and as soon as she did she blocked him on all technology. He would no longer be able to contact her, even if he really needed to.

The Shark was now officially banned from her life.

He came back with his hands up, as if surrendering in a war. And if you knew him you would know that this was a very difficult thing for him – to give in, to admit defeat, to show even the slightest ounce of weakness. It was something he never did, and that was why he was so successful.

But upon his return, the girl had been pitiless. She had been the shark he already knew her to be. She had adopted a no-bullshit tolerance in his absence. Yet winning, shutting the door in his face, didn't come with the satisfaction she had been so convinced it would. The girl had expected happiness, a higher level of **self-worth**, the feeling of a queen defeating a king. And yet she was left with none of that.

Relief and some sort of closure yes, but not happiness. Not a feeling of **accomplishment**.

Because once it's all done and dusted, feeble things such as winning do not matter. The bottom line is two people that care about one another have cut ties forever, and there is nothing sadder than that.

What Followed

Magic

It was 4am in Venice and the city was as magical as ever. The marine had his arm wrapped around the girl as they gazed out at the beautiful buildings that passed them, illuminated by the night lights. It was ridiculously romantic, and the girl was beaming. She breathed in the smell of the polluted water and for the first time in a long time, she felt free. She felt hopeful. That perhaps she could get her life together. That perhaps the pain of being without the Shark could one day be something she could adapt to.

All that could be heard was the engine of the vaporetto running at a slow pace, and the driver near them exchanging sexist jokes with his friend.

This city is amazing, the girl thought to herself as the marine caressed the tip of her shoulder. He had looked after her the entire night, made sure she was always okay. It had been a long time since the girl had been around someone whose primary concern was her.

Caring and humble – are these the qualities they drive into men that join the Navy? Maybe everyone should be made to join then.

The girl turned her head and studied his face; he looked like a model. Once she would show his picture to her friends back in London, they would tell her that he looked like James Franco. He had a chiseled jaw and big, brown cryptic eyes. She couldn't read them, after all, she had only known him two days. She hardly knew anything about him, he was practically a stranger. And yet he had looked after her the entire night. She hadn't asked, she hadn't expected him to, but he had taken it upon himself to be a complete and utter gentleman. It felt good.

He suddenly noticed a bit of mud on her leg from when she had tripped earlier and attempted to rub it off with his hand, the young couple opposite them staring.

How bizarre, the girl thought to herself. *To the outside world we look like a couple, when in reality it's our first and last date.*

"Thanks," she said, softly.

He managed a smile as he released his arm from her, placed himself in front of her and put his hands on her hips. He didn't say a word as he looked into her eyes, but to the girl they seemed to read, 'I really enjoyed meeting you, Skye'.

Well, maybe I can read him a bit after all, the girl thought to herself.

He slowly leaned in, but his lips were not aiming for hers. They were slowly making their way above her lips, above her nose....

No, no, no! Not the forehead kiss! No! Those motherfuckers always get me! No!

But the marine couldn't read her thoughts, and he placed a long and affectionate kiss on the girl's forehead, closing his eyes. The girl inwardly sighed, closing her eyes too, and knowing full well that she was going to be taking this moment with her back to London.

Thank you.
Thank you, you incredibly handsome Italian marine.
Thank you.

Struggle

"Skye?" I heard a stern, male voice say, but I was too focused on trying to understand the witness summons letter on the screen in front of me. I didn't understand a word of it, it was all legal speak that completely and utterly baffled me. "Skye? Hello?"

I looked up to see Will, one of the lawyers at the firm, standing next to me in his cheap suit and an even cheaper briefcase in his hand. "Oh sorry Will..."

"I'm going to court now, are you ready?"

I gulped.

Ok, I have two choices here: A), I could remind him that I have never worked in law before this job, how the hell have you made the decision to take me to court, to a real case, with you? Are you wanting me to embarrass you?

Or B), smile, nod and collect my things, sneaking a legal dictionary into my bag on the way out.

I nodded and got up. My colleague Nancy, a fellow legal administrator, eyed me.

"You'll be fine," she told me with warm eyes.

"Sure," I replied, just as Martin, another lawyer, dumped a very large amount of paperwork on my desk. "For when you get back."

"After court?"

"Yes. Come straight back here please. I need these done by tonight."

I know it's crazy but through all the chaos and stress and freaking out, I was buzzing. And what exactly was the buzz for? Well I figured out pretty quickly that it was for the challenge, the drive, to win at something. It turned out I loved it; I loved the anarchy that ensued to get stuff done. I was stressed beyond words, I was spending all my spare time reading legal books and documents, I was constantly tired, but I was buzzing. I felt I had purpose again. And I was going to become the damn best at my job, even if it killed me.

The Qualities We Search For

I don't know what I look for in a man. It seems after the Shark I am only more confused about my preferences. To reach to his position, the Shark had developed a ruthless character; cold and all about winning. I had seen it in his eyes right from the first time I had seen him, but I had allowed myself to proceed nonetheless. I inevitably paid the price of course, eventually becoming a consequence to his choice of lifestyle.

But there were positives too. He had had the most incredible focus and discipline I had ever encountered in another human being. It had empowered me, inspired me. And to start off with, it had been amazing to be around someone with so much self-motivation; it gives you such a buzz.

But eventually it became toxic, because even though on one side he was a sharp, power hungry man that seemed like he could succeed at anything, on the other side he was a small boy, scared shitless of human interaction. Capable of destroying anyone that tries to tap into that fear.

Anyone.

For me ambition in a man is very important, but I often wonder if I will be able to find that again without paying dire consequences for my preferences. Can you be ambitious and not be selfish? Can you love someone and be successful at the same time? Where do you draw the line?

Because admittedly, despite his dark flaws, he always believed in me and my writing, he always pushed me to be better, to reach my goals. Whether I like it or not he helped me evolve, and that is a quality in a partner I will always desire.

Dating apps are changing the course of dating forever. With casual sex at our fingertips, many of us have become lazy and the concept of dating is rapidly dying. Most men will cheer as they read this, but be careful guys, because this affects you too. With nobody bothering to date anymore, more and more people find themselves in toxic relationships.

Sex creates the illusion of a relationship with no real basis for one, so what does that mean for us? It means more and more of us will wake up after years with someone realising they've been sleeping next to a stranger. If you're after one thing these apps are harmless to you, but if you find yourself in a relationship without having dated the person, you might want to take a minute and reflect on how exactly you ended up there.

The pain I feel in his absence
Is something I've never felt before
It is pure agony
It is my heart aching
For his presence
It is turmoil
In its purest form.

Top Five Signs to Run (He's a Fuckboy!)

1. **If he says 'I'm not an asshole'.** Who are we kidding here? This quote is reserved especially for the smaller brained fuckboys who, not knowing how to trick you, decide to tell you the contrary of what they are.
2. **If he keeps his phone upside down in your presence.** This one is fairly simple: he does not want you to see the kiss and heart emojis from that girl on that dating app whom he has yet to meet but had phone sex with last night whilst you were in the shower.
3. **If he's got a six pack.** Now I don't want to generalise or stereotype but, if he's got a six pack, chances are he's dating one girl for each pack. Mathematically it makes sense. To him, anyway.
4. **If he asks you if you believe in love.** Do I believe in what now?! This one is usually reserved to guys who think we still live in the 1940s and that the sheer mention of the word 'love' will make us take off our panties.
5. **If his profile picture on chat apps is of him topless.** Need I say more? **RUN, WOMAN!** Run as fast as you can...

Teddy and Muggles

We walked down the quiet road in silence, and I looked at the man walking beside me, the street lights illuminating his sad expression. I realised in that moment that this would be the last time we walk anywhere together and it gave me a sad feeling in my stomach.

*What is it about endings that bring about silence? Or perhaps he is in denial, perhaps he has decided to ignore my speech about wanting to be alone, wanting to deal with the pain on my own, **my** way.*

I had a long way to go. Maybe I would never be okay sharing something with another person ever again. Maybe I would end up living on the coast with 15 cats. Maybe I would sit at the beach with Teddy and Muggles and remember him, remember this night.

He fished out his cigarettes. "It was a pleasure to have spent time with you, and to have met you," he told me, a cigarette between his lips.

So he does know it's over. Before it ever really began, to be honest.

"It was a pleasure for me too," I managed to reply. I was glad I had been direct, that I had been able to look him in the eye and tell him how I felt. It may come easy to most people, at least in my circle, but to me it was one of the hardest things in the entire world. I had always been an evasive person, for as long as I could remember. Maybe I was growing.

And I was sad, for the simple reason that I was sad whenever anything came to an end. I guess this was typical of a writer – being sensitive to everything at all times. I was sad in a good way, in a way that wasn't dangerous, like your last day of school, or when you leave home. You know it's time to let go, you know it isn't where you want to be anymore, but you're sad anyway because, even if only for a fleeting second, it was something in your life that had had meaning. It was something that had given you something.

"You are by far the strangest girl I have ever met," he told me. It wasn't vindictive or malicious, it was just plain fact.

I was strange. I had always been strange. And I probably always would be. "I can't wait to see you as a famous writer, that's gonna be funny."

"Who says I'm gonna make it?"

"Oh, you are. You will."

I slipped my hand into his, and we walked hand-in-hand to Earl's Court tube station in silence. This was the first and last time we would ever do this, and there was something strangely melancholic about it. I knew that one day he would be a boyfriend to someone who would appreciate him, who would love him for his kindness. To me he would forever be the-one-that-would-have-made-an-amazing-boyfriend.

I was the asshole. I was the one that never fell in love with the right person, with the one that was right for me. And whilst I imagined his future exploring Tokyo with a pretty and devoted woman, I imagined myself on the beach with Teddy and Muggles, and of course, my notebook.

Well, it doesn't seem so bad.

There is no better trainer than <u>yourself</u>,
There is no greater motivator than <u>yourself</u>,
There is no bigger game changer than <u>yourself</u>.

How are fuckboys so successful with women? I'm not getting it. But I do find their place in society fascinating. Guys with minimal brain cells talking about their morning training regimes and calling you 'baby', thinking you won't be able to resist their steroid-induced bodies. How many times have I been on first dates with one and have sat there bored out of my mind as they talk about social media or what rabbit food they had for breakfast. It's great to be healthy yes, but does it look like I give a fuck about your breakfast, mate? Seriously? Oh and now he's sending me selfies of himself, isn't that nice?

Don't even think for a second you're gonna get an intelligent conversation out of them - dare to bring up Brexit, I double dare you. He'll probably think it's a type of biscuit. Perhaps I'm being slightly harsh, but I personally am not drawn to men who take more selfies than I do or who have the sexual morals of a chimpanzee. But I've been out with douchebags and I've fallen for douchebags, so who am I talk?

Admittedly, fuckboys are a fascinating look at modern dating. When did this become attractive? When did low intelligence, big egos and no respect for women become something we in general as a gender not only allow ourselves to date, but actually find appealing?

The Start

I knew I wanted to be a writer when I was six. Six years old. I remember what I was wearing that first time I picked up a pen with the intention of telling a story. I remember exactly where I was sitting, in which room of my parents' house, and the feeling it gave me to know I was about to create something. That amazing, irreplaceable feeling of making something that is *yours* and *yours only*. I wrote short story after short story, year after year, up until 13. A month after my 13th birthday, I wrote my first novel – it started off as a letter to my brother, and then suddenly it was 176 pages long and funnily enough, no longer following the standard letter format. It was about New York street gangs, and if I'm being honest, it was awful. The structure, the punctuality – all pretty horrendous and inconsistent. But the idea behind it and the characters were incredible. At least to me, anyway. So I wrote a few more novels, all pretty much as awful as each other, give or take a cheesy sentence or two.

Once I began to study literature at college however, it was much easier for me to see where I was going wrong, and develop an actual writing style. At 18, I interned for a pre-production film company, and I remember sitting down to have a one-to-one with one of the producers on my penultimate day there.

"How can I help you, Skye?" asked the very cute Argentinian film producer.

"I think of ideas. Like, every day. About ten a day. Book ideas, film ideas; and I write them down on napkins, tissues, cardboard...I just never seem to remember my damn notebook! And cute little purses don't really fit notebooks, retailers are so inconsiderate!"

He laughed, and rubbed his hands together, looking at me with curious eyes. Being an 18 year old female intern, it was something rare to be taken seriously, to not be looked at with perverse or snobbish eyes, but as if he actually valued you as a person. In fact, out of the entire company he was the only one who took me seriously. Who, when talking to me, looked at me as another human being, and not a small, helpless girl. That was exactly why I had chosen him to have this talk with.

"Skye, you're a writer," he told me.

I liked the sound of that. I liked the sound of that a lot. "Not a producer?"

"No. You come up with the ideas; producers than develop those ideas. It sounds like you like to be the seed."

"I suppose I do."

"Here," he pulled out a brown notebook from his bag. "Have mine. Remember to always carry this, and write down every damn idea you get."

My eyes lit up as he handed me the note book, as if it were Christmas and my birthday all in one. "Oh wow! I can't possibly take this, it's yours!"

He shook his head. "I bought it a couple of days ago, but haven't had a chance to use it yet. I can get another one. This one should be yours."

I beamed at him. "Thank you!"

"Just work on your ideas; develop, develop, develop. Don't be put off by *bad* ideas; we all have them. In fact, most of your ideas will probably *be* bad at first. It'll take a lot of time and effort to make it to the point where you'll think of a good idea. But once you do, it'll feel like gold, I promise you."

It's nine years later that I write this. Nine years. And where exactly am I writing this from?

From my very first blog.

Welcome.

London Girl of Intrigue– that's me.

I'm a writer.

And you better believe...

I AM GOING TO BE THE DAMN SEED.

That sounded sexual when it wasn't supposed to.

Why didn't it sound sexual when the cute Argentinian film producer said it?

You know how I know when a relationship was worth it? You know how I know when it was real? When despite the bad words said, and the childish things done, when you are about to do something big in your life, something important, you can still hear his voice cheering you on.

You can still see that expression on his face that read, 'come on Skye, you can do this'.

It was never a half-assed attempt to appear supportive, and it was never fake. It was a complete 100% belief that I could achieve anything I put my mind to.

And that beats every bad word said, and every childish action taken.

Just don't tell him that.

P.S. I got this.

When I meet personal trainers who are serial cheaters, I am baffled by the hypocrisy. You preach mind control, yet cheat with the excuse of 'I can't help it'.
'<u>I can't help it</u>' is the definition of coward.

Have a Scotch

It's 11:30pm on Sunday night and I know exactly where you are. You're in a bar in Notting hill, Scotch in hand. You're there in your ridiculously expensive Armani shirt and gelled up hair that I detest. It's okay though, because everybody else in this bar is a posh twat too, so you fit right in.

You are unaware of your surroundings, as per usual. Somebody could be dying in front of you and you won't notice. And this is because you're too busy brainstorming and stressing out.

You are incredibly successful for your age, but that's not how you're seeing it. You're only seeing the blank spaces, the things you haven't done yet in order to reach where you want to be. Because your destination changes every other day; your goals become bigger, the challenges more chaotic, just the way you like them. Because without those challenges you would die. Even as you sit there you are thinking of 20 different things you need to do to step up your game and how you're gonna get there.

Relax. You're gonna do it all, and you're gonna do it all in style. Remember that you are capable of anything. Believe in yourself. In those moments of weakness when it is hard to do so, have another Scotch and think about all that you have achieved this year.

Don't dwell.
Don't dwell.
Don't dwell.

Whether you are seeing someone new or you've decided to retreat back to your box, I am sure of one thought you will have today:

I wonder if Skye remembers what day it is.

Happy birthday, Shark.

Camden Town

I sat in my favourite bar in Camden, writing in the corner. People surrounded me, laughing and joking and drinking, but I didn't see or hear them. I was too much in my own world, like I always was when I was writing. When I was brainstorming. When the creative juices were flowing.

"Skye!" a familiar voice screeched, and I looked up to find Sofia approaching, Alfie following. They both had massive grins on their faces, and I shot up, running into Sofia's arms.

"Hey!"

"Hey, girl! *Where* have you been? At last we get to see you! It's been far too long!" Sofia groaned, as I hugged Alfie.

"I know, I'm sorry, I'm sorry, it's been really hectic." We sat down on the comfy sofa chairs that surrounded the rectangular glass table.

"So why have you been so busy? Is it the job? How's it going?"

"Well, yes and no – the job is very hectic, but I'm starting to get a handle on it."

"Do you deal with a lot of paperwork?"

"Yes, but I also get to see how lawyers talk and deal with a whole bunch of things," I told them both, as they smiled back at me.

"So are you going to be a lawyer?"

"No," I said, firmly. "I don't think I'm supposed to be a lawyer. I enjoy what I do, but...no, I'm not supposed to be there."

"I told you! I told you Skye, you're not a legal type. You're a creative type!"

"So what are you going to do?" Alfie asked me, curiously.

"Well, I'm gonna start looking for other jobs, other industries. But, whilst I do that...I am also doing something else."

They both stared at me, waiting for me to elaborate.

"I'm writing a book."

"*What?* Oh, wow!"

"Yes. It's on the music industry, fiction novel, based in London. I actually started it years ago and then...gave up. But now I'm working on it, every day, every evening after work, the weekends..."

"Oh wow, novels take a lot of work."

I nodded.

"You know who you remind me of? Skye...you're becoming like *him*."

I gulped, knowing exactly who she meant.

"I'm not. He was completely different."

"It's the same thing, Skye," Sofia paused, as she studied me. "Have you heard from him?"

I shook my head, keeping my eyes on the shiny floor of the bar. "He's blocked, Sofia. He can't contact me."

"Aren't you curious, though? Imagine he needed something urgently, or if he declared his love for you..."

"No words from him can bring any happiness, it's all poison," I said, and there was silence at our table. I felt as if both Sofia and Alfie were tapping into my pain somehow, and I needed to kick them out. I clapped my hands together. "Anyway! I'm writing a book, guys."

"And we can't wait to read it," Alfie told me, rubbing my shoulder.

I had set up that meet because I was spending too much time alone, too much time working, so much so that I feared I would lose all my friends, and that somehow I needed to be social to feel more normal.

But I didn't. Somehow, being around people, no matter how much I loved them, didn't seem to bring me joy, at least not in that moment. I had so much to do. I had so much to catch up on. I felt alive, and I needed to embrace all my skills, and push myself to be the best I could be. Spending my Friday nights in bars was no longer something on my agenda. I had too much to do, and not enough time to do it all.

I'm sure they will be okay without me for a while.

It is far more the struggle for triumph than triumph itself that gives my life meaning.

When out on dates, I often imagined the Shark there with me. He would pull up a chair next to us in his slick Dolce & Gabbana shirt, and ridiculously gelled up hair. A whiskey in hand, and a big smirk on his face.

"What are you doing, Skye?" he would ask with that confidence that always frustrated me. "You think this jackass can make you happy? Look at him. You have total power over him. Total power bores you. It doesn't hold your attention for a nanosecond. Look at him – taking in your bullshit, not seeing behind the mask. He will never see behind the mask."

"Go away!" I would protest in my head.

"You think he's able to challenge you? To handle you when you're being impulsive? When your darkness comes out?" the Shark would shake his head to accompany his smirk, and raise his glass. "I am the *only* one that can do that. Cheers..."

Solo Traveller

There's this stigma attached to a girl travelling alone, as if it is something absolutely terrible to do. *What kind of impression are you giving other people, Skye?!? Do you want people to think you're a loner? Travelling alone, how absurd!*

The reactions I have received from people I have met along the way include:

How brave!
How odd.
Good for you!
I wish I had the guts to do it!
awkward silence
ALONE ALONE? HOW DOES ONE DO THAT?

The truth is, from the day I started I haven't been able to stop. It began when a relationship ended and more than the relationship itself I was disappointed that I couldn't go to L.A.

But then I stopped and thought, *hang on, if I want to go to L.A., why don't I just go? Why must I sit here twiddling my thumbs, when I could be in L.A. having a grand old time?* (Which I did have).

Why am I waiting for this supposed 'company' that makes me seem 'normal' to society? I've never been particularly 'normal', why start now?

Travelling alone is an adventure different to one when travelling in company. And your connection to the places you visit are truly unique. It's a beyond wonderful experience, as long as you remain vigilant at all times. Yes, it can be dangerous. Yes, I've encountered weirdos along the way, and I have freaked out over things that luckily turned out to be nothing, but I still recommend it. Because whenever I start a solo trip I have this undeniable smile on my face, and I'm ready for my adventure!

Travelling alone is, essentially, the decluttering of the soul.

I know all I have to do is write to him and he will appear. A simple 'hey' and he will reply. I know all I have to say are three words and he will say 'okay'. Those three words are 'I need help' and he's waiting for them to appear on his phone screen.

Putting a book together all by myself is not completely batshit crazy, but it's really difficult. And it's taking up all my time. But I love it, because I love this book.

Admittedly, however, there is sometimes a thought that creeps up on me – the fact that I'm not visually creative like him. I'm good with words, not visuals. People pay for his ideas every day, for his mind, and I could get it for free simply by texting him those three words.

But I refuse, and I will continue to do so indefinitely. Because I can do this alone. And I will.

The Monster

Panic hit, and when panic hit, the girl had to flee the scene as fast as possible.

"Skye, don't. Please. Don't," he told her, standing in front of her in only his boxers. She, on the other hand, was already fully dressed. She grabbed her trainers and put one on, lacing it up. She kept her eyes fixed on the knots she was making, rather than on the man in front of her.

"Skye. Please don't run."

"I told you, right from the start. I told you!"

He kneeled down in front of her. "Skye. Are you listening to me? Let's talk about this like adults. You're always so mature, but when you panic...all that trust you built towards me, trust that took some time to get from you, it disappears. Instantly. Let's talk about this-"

"I don't want to talk about anything! I just want to leave! So get out the way!" the girl saw the monster she was unleashing, but she couldn't stop it. Particular words triggered something in her that made her fire off like this. She was damaged beyond repair, she didn't understand her actions as much as the people around her that cared about her.

She knew it had to do with the Shark, and she began to hate herself for having chosen to pursue that road. She hadn't listened when her gut had told her to walk away, and now she was left with the consequences.

"I know you're in pain. I want to help. I want to help, Skye..."

The girl stared at the naïve man kneeling in front of her. They had been seeing each other only a month but he was besotted. She, on the other hand, was not.

"You can't help. This is something I must do alone."

"You're not going to make it alone, you need someone to help you, to share the pain with you. When we're together I feel your pain, I swear to God, I feel it. I just wanna help you."

The girl rose and said bluntly, "don't text me," before marching out of his flat.

Oh and how it hurt,
To see him and not be seen anymore;
To watch his world
And no longer be a part of it
To learn of his accomplishments
From a picture
Or a sentence on a screen;
Rather than from his lips
Or his eyes
Or his arms
How cruel it was
To have grown accustomed to his scent
And to have to give it up
Indefinitely
And in exchange
Catch glimpses of the life he builds
Without you.

Girls are lucky, they can find their admirers simply by posting a half-assed attempt at a good selfie on social media.

Instinct

I knew he was going to interest me the entire month before we actually met. That's why I stood very nervously at Angel underground tube station that Friday night. We had started chatting on a popular dating app – I was spending too much time working on the book and on myself. I was burning out. I had decided I needed to make time to be social, to take me away from goals and deadlines to get to know another human being. Even if just for one evening every fortnight.

I had gone out on three dates so far – the first had been *way* too desperate for sex, the second had had the most awful laugh imaginable, and the third still lived at home with his parents.

When you live in a city where no one makes eye contact on the tube, you start to understand why so many people choose to use dating apps, even just to meet new people. It's a very fast-paced city, and sometimes, if you're not careful, you can get left behind.

I had never before been nervous about meeting someone from a dating app; I was an expert, always the 'cool cat', leading the conversation and having all power on the situation. Yet somehow I was nervous about meeting the DJ. He had caught my attention with his high level of intelligent conversation and genuine thoughtful comments on my writing and my need to find a new job. I was about to leave mine, and I was looking for my next adventure.

I was changing. I was spending my weekends working on my novel and coming up with plans for the future. I knew this influence was from the Shark, and it made me proud. It felt good to know I had at least taken something noble from him.

But it was also bizarre, as I still felt him with me. More than half a year had passed since I had blocked him on all technology, but I still felt him with me. Every single day. And I wondered how he was, if he was okay, if he was happy. I still researched his career on the Internet about once a month, and had recently discovered he had won the position in NYC he had been dreaming of for years. I wanted to unblock him and congratulate him, ask him when he was moving across the pond, but I knew it wasn't a good idea. It wouldn't be healthy for me. And so I instead lay myself down on my bed, smiling to myself and taking a second to be proud of him.

When the moment passed I simply got up, and carried on with my life.

The DJ:

Skye I'm so sorry, I'm running from my flat to the station! Will be there in 5 minutes!

Skye:

No worries. Make sure you don't go up to the wrong girl!

The DJ:

Haha, but what if she turns out to be the love of my life?

Skye:

Then I shall write a book about it.

I was so nervous I was trembling. *Calm the fuck down Skye, you've done this plenty of times, what's your problem?*

I put my phone away and decided instead to watch people pass through the barriers. It was 9PM on Friday night, two days before Halloween and most people around me were dressed up. They were happy, buzzing, and ready for their big Friday night out. I felt weird and on the outside of it all. I wondered what the DJ would be like, if he would live up to my expectations of him.

The DJ:

Hey.

I instantly looked up, searching the crowd and spotting him instantly. He stood a few metres away, looking straight at me, with a very infectious smile and an attractive, olive-skinned face.

Very cute. Oh no, we already know how this is going to go. Very cute indeed...

His eyes trailed down my jacket, to my skirt, to my shoes, and I hoped he wasn't disappointed with the girl he had been picturing for the past month. I always tried to use pictures that accurately fit my actual appearance. I mean, what's the point of putting up an airbrushed picture of yourself on a dating app? You do realise he will see the real you when you meet, right?

"Hi!"

The conversation, as expected, was awkward for the first half an hour of the evening. I was so nervous I was avoiding eye contact. *That's right Skye, show him how weird and nervous you are – men love that, don't they?*

As we walked side-by-side to the patisserie and shared typical small talk, I noticed from the corner of my eye that he was slightly shorter than I had imagined, but then again I had a long history with dating short men so it didn't bother me. As long as he wasn't shorter than me I could live with not being able to use heels.

The small talk quickly died down and we instead got into conversation as fascinating as our texts had been. It was refreshing to be around someone with ambition and drive. It had been too long. I let it soak in, bathing in the good energy and motivation of the DJ, as he spoke to me about his career.

It was clear he was only on the app for one reason, and my heart made a mental note to remember to not get close to him. I just wanted to be around the good vibes that he was providing me with.

It was three or four hours later that we sat opposite one another in some dark bar in Shoreditch, no table between us, conversing with one another only inches from each other's faces. And I realised, as we smiled and shared stories with one another, that this was the first time in a long time that I was genuinely interested in another person.

As I told the DJ stories about my Sicilian adventures, it was like I was uncovering the social side to me that I had locked away six months ago.

"Good!" the DJ said once I told him this. "You need to relax sometimes, Skye."

I told him I had to leave at about midnight as I had an 'early start' but it was total rubbish. I simply didn't want to drink too much and end up dancing especially close to him on the dance floor. There was definitely chemistry.

He had to stay, his friend was playing a set downstairs, and so he walked me out of the bar and waited with me for my taxi. We looked around at the vibrant Friday night in Shoreditch that surrounded us.

"So...it was really good to meet you," he told me and I smiled.

"You too."

"Maybe if we find some time on our busy schedules to meet again, we will?" It was more a question than anything else.

"*Well*, I can't guarantee anything," I joked, but inside I hoped he would text me tomorrow.

For no particular reason at all, I decided to playfully punch him on the shoulder.

"Don't make me start, Skye."

"Go on, give me your best shot. You know I do boxing, right?"

He suddenly locked my arms behind my back. "You were saying, Skye?" Some people passing us looked on, wondering what the hell we were doing. He spun me around slowly and I giggled.

"You realise I can get out of this in a second?"

He let me go and we faced one another, just as my taxi pulled up in front of us.

It's time to go, Skye. Is he going to kiss you? Come on, kiss me...I want you to. Just a small kiss.

But before I knew it, he pulled me into a bear hug. It had been so long since I had been held so tightly. I had forgotten how much I liked it and missed it. I put my arms around him and hugged him just as tightly.

Once we let go, he smiled sweetly at me. "Goodnight, Skye."

Looking into his big, hazel eyes, I knew that we both wanted the same thing. The attraction was there, and it was strong. But I wondered, and I feared, if perhaps I would develop an emotional attachment to him for the completely wrong reasons.

But without obsession, nothing really great gets done, does it?

Sometimes I imagined what it would be like to tell him.

"I write about you. Like all the time. It has everything about us. It has your expressive eyes, your curved smile, your nervous habits. My female readers are obsessed with you."

"You're writing about me? Like we promised so long ago?"

I imagined how he would look at me, I imagined that strength being transported to me like it always used to, empowering me and making me feel like I was capable of anything. I remembered that belief he had had in me as a writer, I remembered his words, words that have stuck with me as permanent as my tattoo.

"You're a writer, Skye. Always have been, always will be," said with such sincerity and zero doubt, said as if they were simply plain fact.

I have only been in love once. I have only ever been affected by *one* person in my life up until now. How crazy is that? Or maybe it's sad. I am such a difficult character, such a loner, such a fucking weirdo.

So many kisses, so many shared silences, yet there is only one person in the entire world up until now that I have been perfectly content sitting on a cold kitchen floor with at 4AM.

He came in like a storm. He was the most interesting person I had ever known. And he changed everything.

The Return

After imagining it in my head for months, there he was, standing in the distance. All the times I had left the office and looked around the entrance hoping to see him standing there, waiting for me, wearing one of his overly expensive suits and ridiculously gelled up hair. I often imagined what he would say.

"I need to talk to you, Skye!" he would shriek in desperation, because that's what people in love did – they shrieked things at you, and the urgency in their voice would jump out at you, trying their damn hardest to grab your attention.

But that never happened. Every evening I would leave work secretly disappointed, and as time went by, I eventually gave up on the fantasy.

But now he was here, in the flesh, waiting for me. Seeing the Shark without any warning whatsoever made my stomach tighten instantly.

What the hell is he doing here?!

He looked nervous – prancing up and down the entrance of my building. It's crazy how your body reacts when a face you love with every being of your existence suddenly appears in front of you. My stomach was doing somersaults, and I was instantly trembling.

He noticed me and I immediately turned around, trying to flee the scene as fast as possible.

"Skye..."

That voice...

"Skye!" he caught up with me and stopped in front of me. "Stop, hold on, please. Just listen."

I froze in my spot. I hadn't seen him in ten months, and his face seemed older. It was a little cleaner shaven than it used to be, and his eyes were different. A little less dark.

I pulled my scarf up to my nose, as if purple wool was going to protect me from the toxic asshole standing in front of me.

"How are you?"

"What do you want?"

The Shark took a deep breath in, thinking carefully about how he should respond. "Last time we spoke...you blocked me before I even had a chance to reply."

"I was really angry, you know this. Anything you would have said would have only upset me further," I told him, and he searched my eyes the way he used to whenever I would try to hide my emotions.

You're not going to see that you still have an effect on me. You're not. These eyes will not reveal a thing!

"I'm sorry," he suddenly said, "I'm sorry for everything. My intention was never to hurt you, you know this. Skye, you know this. You were...you are...I'm sorry."

I couldn't believe it. The man standing in front of me had never apologised for anything in his entire life. He was the arrogant, successful city slicker who could never do no wrong. He was an asshole by nature, and he never deemed this something to be sorry for. But looking at his face and hearing the sincerity in his voice, I felt, for the first time, like perhaps I had given him something. And it was the most beautiful feeling in the world.

I pulled down my scarf. "Thank you," I managed to reply, without any animosity in my tone. I felt something leave me, something dark, as soon as I heard those words come out of his mouth. It left my soul and floated into oblivion.

There was silence between us and I had chills on the back of my neck. We stared at one another for what seemed like an eternity before he spoke again.

"I'm glad you're fine. I did it, by the way – I won a place, and it was all because of the biography *you* wrote me."

I forced my eyes to light up, to pretend as if this was news to me.

"You're going to New York?"

"Yes."

Suddenly I wasn't remembering the times we had hurt each other, all the pain we had caused one another. I was instead remembering us inspiring each other to be better, to keep going, telling each other we could do it, picking each other up when the other was falling to pieces. I was proud of the achievements of the person standing in front of me as much as I would be if the accomplishments were mine. It was a very bizarre feeling.

"Oh my God, congratulations! Wow, that's amazing..."

"Thank you, thank you so much. You made this happen Skye, you were there beside me and you know how much it means to me. Thank you so much."

I wanted to hug him, I really did, even after everything. But I didn't, I held back with all the resistance I could muster. Love is stupid. It makes you forgive the cruellest of things. It makes you remember only the good memories, and you let them linger in your soul as an excruciatingly painful reminder of the happiness you once experienced. You forget the things that ripped your soul to shreds, and just see someone that had once made you very happy. You are a person in love. And a person in love is never rational.

"Can I take you for a coffee? I would really like to catch up."

A coffee? I must seem cool and collected on the outside, he must think I've moved on with my life the way he probably has. He doesn't know that I write pieces about him every other day. That I remembered his birthday. That I research his career progress and already know he had got the job he wanted. No I can't go for coffee with him, I need to get out of here.

"I actually have to get home and work on the book."

"The book? You're doing it?"

"Of course. All I do is work, day and night. I don't go out, I just work. Definitely got this influence from you."

"Oh my God, I'm honoured! Wow."

"I guess I should thank you too – for influencing me the way you did."

"It was a pleasure, Skye. And anyway, I didn't do anything – you already had it in you, I just gave you a little push," we smiled amicably at one another. I had a sudden montage of flashbacks like a kick to the stomach. Yet each moment with him felt like it was part of someone else's life, or scenes from a film I had watched.

"I'd better get home and to work – don't want to get behind on deadlines."

"Oh wow, this is incredible. Well done, Skye. Keep going. Don't ever give up, okay? If I have to give you just one piece of advice it's that. If I'm successful it's because I never gave up. And look, I just about made it."

"Never doubted you for a second."

"I know you didn't," he paused, "text me when you want to get that coffee, I think we should. It was really nice seeing you. You've made me very happy knowing that I was any part of the person you are becoming."

Trembling, I smiled and walked away. I walked away imagining myself unblocking him on all technology. I walked away imagining myself sitting opposite him in a posh café in Notting hill, drinking coffee as we updated each other on our lives. I could see it. I could see myself remaining in love with the asshole for the rest of my life.

But little did I know that none of that would happen. That seeing him, and hearing 'I'm sorry' had set me free. That his power over me had turned to dust. That after that day I would stop searching his name on the Internet, I would stop wondering how he was. I didn't know it yet, but that night, I let him go. And I let all the ghosts go with him.

That silence in your life after you lose someone you care about – no matter how it happens; death, heartbreak, stubbornness. It leaves an unexplainable void, one that I'm inclined to believe never leaves us; we simply adapt to it.

It's almost as if we were not made to deal with such things.

Tiramisù

The DJ cooked me dinner for our second date, and we sat at the candle lit table for hours, talking non-stop about anything and everything. We got on well, and never seemed to shut up, but if I'm honest, that night I longed for him to kiss me. Physical contact seemed like an impossibility, sitting all the way across the table from me I felt as if we were a million miles apart. I watched his lips as he spoke passionately about the music business and everything else we had in common, but I longed for those lips to be on me. I wondered what it would feel like, if his slight shyness would disappear, melt into oblivion, or if he would be awkward and I would have to lead. Something told me he was the former, but I couldn't be sure. He had shown signs of sheer confidence throughout the evening, but I could tell he was trying hard to keep his guard up.

He was slightly reserved when he spoke, out of shyness rather than disinterest, but it was his mind that had me captivated. I was working 15 hours a day, I wasn't seeing my friends, I didn't have time for anyone, but I had made the DJ an exception. And this was for the sole reason that he was ambitious and driven. Okay that's technically two reasons, but he was those things because he liked to educate himself in every project he got involved in. He read books on anything and everything, to add another power to his already fierce character. I loved it, and more than anything else, I loved that he did it all without any element of arrogance. He was humble, most of the time, and it was a nice change from the Shark.

Our evening passed by in what seemed like a flash, and dinner had gone very well. But at about midnight I decided it was time to give up and go home. He was not going to kiss me.

"I think it might be time for me to leave," I told him, and I could see the disappointment in his eyes.

*Well if you don't make a move, **you're** going to be the one that misses out.*

"Oh, okay, yeah, sure."

I rose, and he followed, not half as enthusiastically.

"Enjoy the tiramisù by the way," I told him,

remembering that the dessert I had made him was still in the fridge.

"Oh shit, your tiramisù! I forgot! Let's have it now!"

"I can't - strict regime. I made it for you."

"Okay, I'll have a piece now, before you go!"

As soon as we approached the kitchen top, the sexual tension hit maximum level. There was no longer a table between us, and we stood next to one another with our arms just about touching. Sparks were flying left, right and centre, but I only stared at the Italian dessert, choosing to ignore it. I was ignoring it because I wasn't sure if it was all one-sided. *Does he want me? He didn't tried anything on the first date, and now here we are at the end of our second one.*

He got out a spoon and offered it to me, but I politely declined.

"Sure? Ok, let's try the tiramisu." There was silence in his flat and all you could hear was the DJ scooping up a corner of the cake. As he picked it up, he suddenly stopped the forkful of tiramisu just inches from his mouth, dropped the cutlery, turned to me and kissed me.

Taken aback, I kissed him back just as passionately. We grabbed each other's faces and gave in to the electricity running between us.

The fire between us only got hotter, and we crashed into the kitchen top as we explored each other's bodies. All those hours of wanting to touch him, to feel his lips on mine, to feel his lips *everywhere* on me, and now it was all exploding...

After a few minutes, I suddenly let go. The DJ and I stood opposite one another, exasperated.

"Wow, Skye...that was...I mean...wow."

"I know."

I knew what he wanted to say next. He wanted to say 'shall we take this upstairs?' That's why I made sure to speak first.

"I should go."

His eyes widened. "What?"

"I've gotta get up early tomorrow...."

We instantly kissed, and crashed into the kitchen table

this time as we let the chemistry take over once more. "I'm gonna...call a taxi," I said, in-between kisses.

"Sure," the DJ replied, as we continued to explore one another. As I kissed him, I managed to grab my phone off the kitchen table, unlocking it and finding the app to call my taxi. The DJ noticed and stopped.

"Oh you're really calling it?"

"Indeed I am."

"You think I'm gonna let you go?" he told me, as he kissed my neck.

"You will have to – I just ordered one." Again we let go of one another and stood watching each other, completely out of breath.

"You're crazy," he told me. "*Why* are you leaving?"

"To drive you insane." It was true. This was only our second date. I was not easy. Playing the game was more fun, more tortuous. I liked to see him squirm. I was squirming too, it was difficult for me to leave, believe me, but I knew it would be worth it.

Always make it painful for them.

"Taxi's arriving in four minutes, you gonna walk me to the door?" I asked him.

"Sure," he paused, "in four minutes though..."

Again we pounced at one another, I wrapped my legs around him and he picked me up, placing me on his kitchen top as we continued to discover one another.

I like this chemistry.

"You don't believe in yourself," the Shark used to tell her. "This is the truth. I can see it, and if anyone else looks close enough, they will be able to see it too. But you know the best solution for this? It's not to hide the truth, but to change the truth.

You are a Shark the same as me, trust me, and that Shark is just waiting to burst out. But in order to find her, you have to learn where to look. It's a process, but I guarantee that one day, your answer to the question 'what do I want?' will no longer be 'I don't know'."

Have a Good Day

I stood next to the coffee machine at work as I scanned over an appeal letter I had just drafted.

"Hey, is Will here?" I heard a voice say. I looked up to see Matthew Walker, a top lawyer from a rival firm standing at reception. Sarah, our receptionist, rang Will's extension number but I already knew nobody would pick up. I walked over to them.

"Will's in court this morning." I told them, both heads turning to me.

"Hey Skye, it's quite important – do you know when he'll be back?"

"Probably not until 2 or 3pm, can I help you with something?" I offered my assistance already knowing his response.

"I need Will, someone legally qualified, Skye." He almost sneered as he told me this, and I was very tempted to throw my coffee in his face. However, I knew there were better ways to crush him.

"No problem, just let me know the issue and I can pass the info onto him."

"Fine. Simon Trevor is one of our clients, and Will poached him. He can't do this, he's still legally ours-"

"Have you spoken to your client?"

"No he's not picking up his phone but-"

"And when was the last time you had communication with him?"

"A couple of weeks back-"

"Right. Well, are you aware that if a client wishes to find new legal representation he is well within his rights to do so?"

"Yes Skye, I know the law, but it wasn't approved by a Judge-"

"I happen to know that it was, since I drafted the outcome of that particular court date."

I watched the blood drain from Matt's face. "What?"

"Yes, and no one from your firm attended that court date, despite the *three* notifications we sent out beforehand."

"I never heard anything-"

"We sent it out via recorded delivery, so if you wish to enquire about the validity of our notifications I will be more than happy to send you proof."

Matt gulped, unsure how to reply. In all the times I had seen him defending in court, I had never seen him speechless. Sara was beaming beside me, impressed by my work.

"I've got to head back to work now, but be sure to pop me an email if you would like me to send them over. Was great seeing you, Matt!"

What a beautiful feeling, to think that somewhere my next adventure awaits.

Change

I was finding that the Shark had been right about a few points – one being that people talked an awful lot about trivial things. Crap that simply did not matter or did not directly affect me in any way, shape or form. Somehow over night, spending time with my friends had become insignificant. I much preferred working on my book – I just needed to find a publishing contract and boom! I would be a published writer in my own right. I also much looked forward to being a published author who used the word 'boom'.

Becoming a published writer had been my dream since I was a kid, since I told my big brother I wanted to be a writer and he told me writers didn't have an easy life.

"I don't care, I will write and I will get paid – I will never stop writing," seven-year-old me told him, to which he had smiled and said, 'then go for it little sis, but be prepared to work hard for it.'

I had recently started writing about the Shark on my blog, and the reaction I was getting was out of this world. At first it was only friends who were following me, and they were telling me they *loved* the pieces on the Shark. I assumed that this was because they knew the real story and liked how I was able to capture it on paper. But soon enough I started getting new followers, followers who didn't know my friends or I – they simply liked my writing, and liked reading about the Shark. It felt pretty damn nice – to have people like what you write. That's essentially the dream come true – for people to connect with your art. It only further motivated me to keep writing.

As for my day job, I chose to work at the law firm because I wanted to see if I could do it. I wanted to see if I could swim when pushed in the deep end, like the Shark had always said I could. And he had been right. At first it had been really difficult, but with some time, patience and hard work, I became stronger than my weaknesses. I learnt to fight against them, and to work on them constantly. I had started drawing up objectives for myself every week, and going through them every Sunday. I became a very self-reflective person, and my drive for success went through the roof. I understood that I wanted more from life, from *my* life. And I was working hard to achieve my goals, to carve a path for myself.

And as interesting as my job was, the challenge was slowly disappearing. I had conquered it, I could feel myself searching for something new, and I knew by then that the field of law was not for me. I wanted to do something creative. My theory was that my drive to succeed could only be consistent if I were to work in something creative. And something happened when I first had this thought – I was suddenly terrified. Just as all people are, when faced with the thought of change. But there was also another feeling that accompanied that fear, and one I had never experienced before under such circumstances – I was excited. It was a feeling of exhilaration that told me:

I am raring to go.
I am alive.
I am ready to conquer the world.

There is a certain satisfaction that comes with writing about the feelings you once had for someone undeserving.

You tap into the moment knowing those feelings no longer exist.

And so you roam around freely, being careful not to touch anything, and safe in the knowledge that the future version of yourself is **stronger, bolder, better** than what you were.

Strange Reality

I was so tired when I finished work, and yet so happy. Wait, there's a better word than that to describe this feeling – what is it?

Satisfied. That's it! I was satisfied. I had quit my old job, and six weeks later, found one I wanted, one I liked – I was a junior art director for an advertising company. It wasn't writing but it was something new, it was something creative, and it was challenging.

I was a step closer to what I wanted to do. I was doing something I enjoyed, and commuting to a cool part of London every morning. Always bouncing with joy, a fruit smoothie in my hand and a smile on my face. I was also back to avoiding sugar and eating super healthy. No more chocolate biscuits. And it felt great.

One autumn evening, I stood at the northbound platform of Baker Street at 6:20pm, reading Albert Camus' 'The Stranger' as I waited for my train. The platform was not as packed as it would have been half an hour earlier, and that was because I had stayed behind briefly to finish something off and had missed peak rush hour. I didn't mind staying behind; I enjoyed my work. And I enjoyed working hard to see results. It came with a satisfaction that brightened my day and gave me a reason to get up in the morning. It was good. Life was good.

"Excuse me..." a shy, girly voice suddenly said. I looked up from my book to see an embarrassed girl in her early twenties with a high ponytail standing in front of me. The ponytail stood out more than anything else as it collided with the strong wind, and my train approached.

"Hi?" I said, expecting her to ask me where Madame Tussauds was or Sherlock Holmes' house. Tourists loved me.

"I don't think you should get back together with the Shark."

I frowned. *What did she just say?!?* The train stopped and the doors opened in front of us.

"*This is Baker Street station. Please mind the gap*

between the train and the platform," the speaker blared, whilst my eyes remained fixed on the girl, stunned.

"I know he helped you evolve – he was a good influence, but I think his dark side will always hurt you. By the way, I love how you write, London Girl of Intrigue"

The blog. She reads my blog. She recognises me from my profile picture. She reads my pieces. She's read all my pieces about the Shark, pieces where I've admitted I still think about him, that I still imagine what it would be like to reunite, to live happily ever after.

"Thank you," I managed to reply, just as I heard the beeping of the doors and instinctively jumped on the train, leaving the stranger at the platform, smiling at me through the double doors.

Damn it, why did I just do that?!

Blame it on being brought up in London, but when I heard tube doors beeping my automatic reaction was to jump on. Even if I didn't want to. Even if it wasn't my train. Except that it had been my train, it was just that I hadn't wanted to leave that moment. I had wanted to talk to her some more, find out what she liked and disliked about my writing. I hadn't wanted to leave that precious moment where someone recognised me for my work. No, wait, where someone *liked* my work. Enough to come over and give me advice. To talk about the Shark as if she knew him. As if she knew our story like a book she had read.

Could I make this a book?

Maybe release it before the novel on the music business?

Is this good enough to be a book?

I remained frozen on the tube for the remainder of my journey, completely and utterly stunned that a *fan* had just approached me.

An actual *fan* of my writing.

And nothing, truly nothing, had ever felt quite as rewarding as that moment.

The trouble is, to be a good writer you must sometimes tap into feelings you probably don't want to tap into.

The Wall

The DJ and I were lying next to one another in the darkness of his bedroom. I was lying on my side, staring at his wall, remembering our first night together just a week earlier. As always, sleeping with someone I didn't love was practically impossible, and I had spent the entire night staring at that damn yellow wall and counting the dots. 98 altogether, if you wanted to know.

There was silence between us but it was the good type of silence, the type that warmed your heart and sent shivers down your spine at the same time. It had been a good evening; we had spoken for hours and hours about music and London and relationships. And all of it in-between kisses and laughter. I felt good. It seemed we were never able to shut up; there was always something to say, something to debate, something to playfully argue about.

We had celebrated my new job with champagne and chocolate cake – his idea.

"I'm really proud of you," he had told me with his arms wrapped around me, nuzzling at my neck. In that moment I half-wished it was the Shark saying it to me, but I shook it off. I needed to let him go now. It was time.

It was 3AM, we had drunk too much and got into way too deep and personal conversations for two people that still did not know each other very well. We were both surprised at the words and thoughts coming out of our mouths, at how we were able to be so honest with each other when usually we were two very defensive people.

I turned to lie on my back and he rubbed my leg.

"I like that we can talk," his voice was low and serious. I wondered if he would have been able to admit this if he had been completely sober. "I like it a lot."

"Me too," I managed to reply, closing my eyes to take in the moment. This was the first moment, since the Shark, that I felt good with another human being. I was scared, terrified, of ending up in the same situation, of perhaps one day writing pieces about the person sleeping next to me. But this feeling, of happiness, of connecting with another being, it was something I could not deny herself. It was rare. It made me feel human. And for this, it would always be worth it. It had to be.

Refusing to let go of something that is not worthy of you, is refusing to make room for something that is.

Thank You

I waited outside the Shark's workplace in the freezing cold with my scarf up to my nose. It felt as if the last time I had stood there had been a 100 years ago.

He strolled out at the exact same time I had expected him to stroll out, dressed in his favourite navy blue Paul Smith suit, the one he always wore when we went out for dinner, accompanied by that same Shark smile he always had. I caught his eye and his smile curved slightly. He tried to hide his apprehension the same way he used to – with substantial effort but never, ever enough to fool me.

"Well hello, stranger." The term was justifiable - we *were* practically strangers now. It was funny, since I had spent more than a year with the person standing in front of me. I knew his body better than my own. So much for *Skye doesn't do love* – it turned out I did, and of course with none other than one of the biggest Sharks in London. It seemed lovers came and went, but I only fell in love with the emotional masochists incapable of loving themselves.

"I know it was you who set up the meeting with the publisher. Thank you."

He searched my eyes the way he used to, except I now no longer tried to hide anything. To the rest of the world I was a mystery; a weird, defensive, unexplainable mystery. But to him I was an open book.

"You're welcome."

Looking into his eyes I realised that I would forever appreciate his ridiculously heavy influence. It was a part of me now, a permanent part of my existence.

I began to walk away.

"Skye..."

I turned around.

"I didn't do it because I owe you anything. I did it because you're a good writer."

Some say that she saved him, whilst others believe it was the Shark who had done the saving.

The truth is, there had been no heroism. No knight in shining armour, and certainly no damsel in distress.

They had simply been two people that had made each other **better**. They had both strengthened the other's weaknesses, pushed the other to evolve, and strived for **more** as a result of one another.

No hero necessary; just the love of someone you admire fiercely.

The Promise

I had become a post-it note nerd. I had them everywhere. I had lists everywhere. Priorities for the day, the week, the month and the year. For work, for the book, my personal goals. I was on fire. I was starting to win at my new job and the feeling was something completely out of this world. For the first time since the music business, I enjoyed my job. I woke up with a smile on my face, with a game plan, with a goal for the day.

After a very successful client lunch, I walked back into the office with a grin and an ere of confidence I was sure that a few months ago did not even exist.

I sat down at my desk, and had three minutes before my next meeting. I quickly checked my email, and noticed an unfamiliar name on one. I opened it up curiously, and it took all of five seconds for me to start grinning from ear-to-ear.

"What's up, Skye? You look happy," said Ryan, a colleague of mine, as he passed me.

"I just got offered the role of editor for an indie online music publication."

Ryan frowned, stopping in front of my desk. "Oh, that's exciting! Congratulations! Does that mean you're leaving us?!"

"Oh no, no – it's a job on the side. I will edit other writers' articles, and if I want to/have time I can write a piece or two myself, go scouting for a few bands..."

"Oh, fabulous! Well, let me know when you write your first piece, I'll check it out!"

"Will do!"

As Ryan walked away, I smiled to myself for the remaining 90 seconds before my meeting.

I told you I wouldn't completely leave you.
I bloody told you.

One of the perks of being a girl is that when your wine glass is empty, there is always someone ready to fill it up.

Verona Train Station

The girl could barely contain her excitement as she stood at the platform at Verona train station. She was grinning from ear-to-ear like a crazy person, dragging her luggage back and forth as she pranced about. The girl couldn't remember the last time she had felt such excitement. It was as if her my insides were dancing around in joy, unable to keep her still. It was -2 outside and just gone 10AM; logic told her she should be miserable. The smoke coming out of her mouth told her she should be freezing to death in her tiny (but adorable) dress. Yet she couldn't feel the cold. Happiness defied the cold. She was on an adventure. Both the DJ and the girl were in Italy over New Year's, and had decided to meet up. Verona was middle ground for both of them, and so they had decided that that would be their destination to spend a couple of days together.

The girl's 6AM start had had nothing on her; she had woken up with a massive smile on her face. Her aunt had thought she was having some sort of stroke.

Her phone suddenly sounded.

The DJ:
The train is just pulling in!!

Skye:
I know!!

Still gleaming, she put her phone away and pranced about the platform a little more as Italians around her stared. She spotted the train approaching and her grin only grew wider, hurting her jaw now.

No longer able to hold back her excitement, she powerwalked to the end of the platform, looking into each of the windows as the train slowly came to a halt. The doors opened as she got to the end of the train, and people came flooding out.

Angry, anxious Italians, bloated from all the Panettone from Christmas and New Year flew passed her in agitation.

"Watch it!" she squealed at one, her massive Cheshire grin never leaving her face and only making her look even more psychotic.

The DJ:
I'm on the platform!! Where are you?

Skye:
I'm here too!

Too exhilarated to elaborate, the girl decided to put her phone away and complete her mission without the help of her phone. There was a certain magic to it. She powerwalked down to the other side of the platform, eyeing every single person rushing past her, from the 70-year-old man blowing his nose, to the pregnant lady screaming down the phone to someone.

The girl continued eyeing everyone until she eventually spotted him in the distance. Wearing his nerdy reading glasses that he claimed were not actually for reading but for his 'fragile green eyes' in the sunlight, he spotted the girl at the exact same moment that she spotted him. In his hands he carried two books, only further reminding her of his peculiarly polygamous relationship with books. This was of course by no understatement one of the things the girl liked most about him.

His grin was just as wide as hers, and just as anxious.

What the hell are we doing here? The girl asked herself. But she soon fly-kicked all panic and worries to the back of her mind. The girl deserved to be happy, even if only for a nanosecond. They both did.

Unable to hold back any longer, she ran into his arms and gave him a sweet kiss on the cheek. He welcomed her arms, pulling her close to him, so that they were cheek-to-cheek.

"We're in Verona. Together. This is so weird," he said in her ear.

Tell me about it, she said to herself.

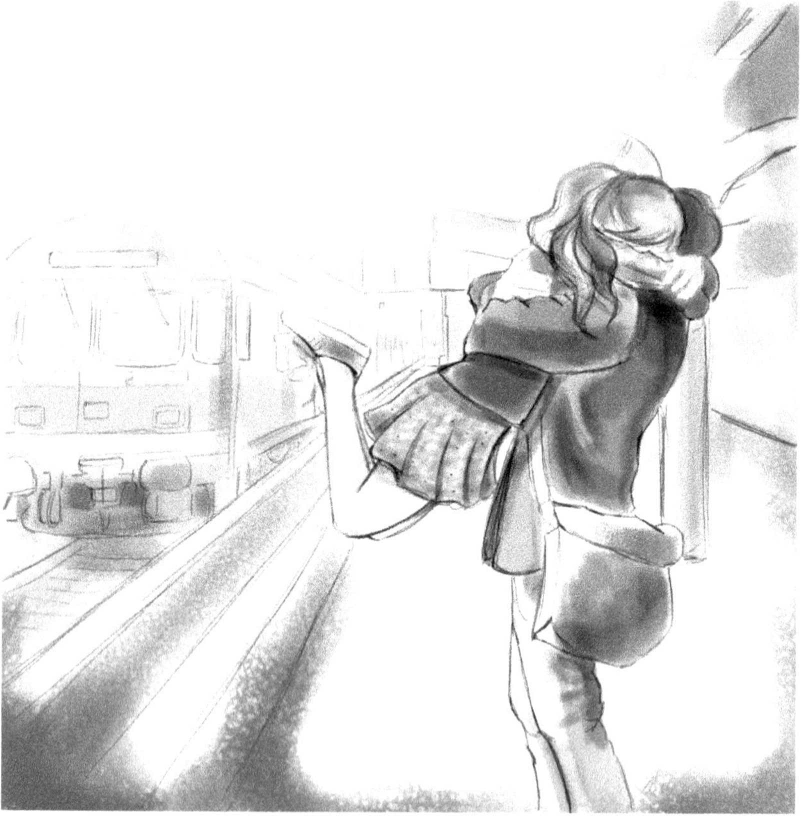

If I had known that letting you go would feel this good, I would have done it a long time ago.

I think sometimes we underestimate our strength, and in doing so, we stand to gain nothing. I have now re-acknowledged the appropriate measure of my worth, re-captured it, and put it back in its cage. And it shall remain with me this time, as permanent as my tattoo.

Romeo to Juliet

The girl dragged her luggage through the pebbled streets of Verona awkwardly, as the DJ told her a story, just as awkwardly. The atmosphere was tense, nothing like when they were in London. It was as if they were strangers that had just met at Verona train station. She thought back to how different it had been when they had last met up two weeks ago and how comfortable they had been in each other's company.

The DJ had this look in his eyes sometimes – like he couldn't believe just how much he was sharing. She imagined a thought bubble appearing above his head reading 'AM I REALLY TELLING HER ALL OF THIS?'

The DJ finished his story and she forced a laugh, hoping it would break the tension. It did not.

What is wrong with us? Have we lost what made us click? The girl asked herself. *I had been so happy to see him at the train station, but now...*

The DJ suddenly put a hand over hers to take her luggage from her.

"Hey, I'll take it."

"No it's fine-"

"No, come on."

In fear of hurting his manhood, the girl let go of her luggage and he took over. They walked beside one another in silence; all that could be heard were the Italians around them conversing loudly with one another, and the girl's luggage being dragged behind them, pebble after pebble.

They had never been awkward, nor had they ever walked in silence. They were two people that, when in each other's company, never seemed to shut up. Discussing books or art or creative people they were envious of, there was always a thousand things to talk about. And when they were apart there were always a thousand things to say via messages, too. Yet there they were, in a new city together, walking beside one another just as awkwardly as when you were paired up with the person you've never said two words to in school.

Why is Verona doing this to us?! It's not like we ended

up in a super romantic city like Venice or Paris! It's Verona! Nothing romantic about this place! The girl said to herself.

She noticed that the DJ had stopped walking and was peering down a narrow street. He suddenly turned to her. "It's Romeo and Juliet's house. Wanna see it?"

"Sure!"

Making their way down the narrow street, they gasped as they took in the walls and walls of handwritten dedications of love. Couples that had travelled across the continent and across the world to write on these walls, to tell the world who they held dearest in their heart. The girl kept repeating to herself 'this is not romantic' as they walked further and further down the narrow street, until they found themselves in front of Romeo and Juliet's house, and more importantly, Juliet's balcony. A shy American teenage girl stood at the edge of it, looking down at her friends, who stood giggling in front of us.

"Oh, Romeo! Romeo! Where for art thou Romeo?" she called, and the girl gulped. She looked around at the crowd, and spotted a couple kissing. Another couple kissing. And another. And another. Panic took over. Her stomach filled with nerves, and she glanced at the DJ.

"Well, this is super weird," he said.

Oh shit, she thought to herself. *We're stuck together for two days in one of the most romantic cities in Italy. What the FUCK were we thinking?*

"Let's get out of here," the girl said, feeling very uncomfortable. The DJ followed, and she felt a little better once they reached the street, and she took a deep breath in.

Again they walked down the street in silence, and the girl tried not to panic about what lay ahead. She was freaking out over the thought of spending two whole days together with this insane awkwardness. *Maybe you could say you have to go home? Pretend to break your leg? Oh please, you two never bullshit each other – just be truthful.*

Just then, amidst the tension between the pair, they passed a man selling roses. "A rose for your beautiful girlfriend?"

Oh no, oh no, oh no! Why are you trying to add to our

awkwardness?! The girl said to herself.

"Actually, my wife and I have to get back to our kids – the babysitter has to be off somewhere," the DJ replied. The girl's eyes widened, but the man with the roses only smiled back at them.

"Beautiful couple! I understand, I have the same problem."

"Yes! A good babysitter is hard to find! Bye!"

As soon as they turned the corner, they both burst into laughter.

"What the hell was that?!" The girl asked him, in-between laughter.

"Well everyone is gonna think we're a couple anyway, might as well have some fun with it!"

The thought of them as a couple made the girl chuckle; they were far too awkward and far too new to one another for any of that. But she suddenly realised that the tension between them was gone. What united them and made them happy to be in one another's company was their humour, and their connection to the outside world. They had very similar output.

"Next person we meet we are acrobats from Finland, okay?" the girl told him, as they began walking again.

"Oh boy."

"And we met when your half brother, Antero, nearly got eaten by a lion at the circus tryouts."

"You're so weird."

"You're not particularly normal yourself."

"Definitely still less weird than you," the DJ told her.

"Fine, I'll take that."

That's the thing i've noticed about kind people — they find much more value in the act of kindness, than in making sure they are being recognised for it.

Knowing

The DJ carried the girl's luggage up the stairs to platforms 8 and 10 of Verona train station. There was an undeniable sadness to the girl as they walked up those stairs. They were about to go in two separate directions. The DJ was off to Milano, and the girl to Bolzano. Verona had united them, but would soon separate them. After 48 hours together, in which they had shared some amazing meals, walked around the city telling each other stories, and climbed pretty high up to look down at Verona in mutual awe, their Veronese adventure was coming to an end. And as travelling tended to do, both of them felt a little different from the two people they had been when they had first started their escapade. It seemed a lifetime ago now, when in reality they had reunited at this very train station only two days earlier.

The girl had decided a few hours into their excursion that in their last hour she would end it, because she had to. Because she knew she wanted different from 2017. She wanted to achieve certain goals and she couldn't do that by continuing to see the DJ. She wanted to be happy, and she knew she couldn't be with him – she needed to stop dating and focus on herself. And the girl knew the DJ didn't like her either, not in the way a girl deserved to be liked.

Yet on that last hour of their trip it had proven impossible for the girl to go through with. She had sat on the bed listening to him sing under the shower in happiness, and smiled as she packed. The happiness in his voice was because of their trip. Of their time together shutting out the rest of the world. And she knew she couldn't do it. Not then. Not in that city.

"I'm platform 8!" the DJ told the girl, as they reached the top of the stairs. "That's my train!"

"I'm platform 10," they both looked at one another. "Where's platform 9?!" they said in synch, followed by laughter.

The girl thought how poetic life could be sometimes – it was as if their trains were on adjacent platforms by purpose, to make their goodbye even more whimsical. Platform 8 had been taken out of existence purely to give them this moment.

"So..." they stood opposite one another in the cold and darkness, nervously studying one another. It was just as cold as when the girl had been waiting for him at the platform 48 hours earlier, only this time she was not immune to it. No, this time the icy cold wind felt crueler, and her legs were starting to tremble.

He handed the girl her luggage. "...amazing trip, Skye. I guess I'll see you back in London...maybe."

"Sure," she lied. And she didn't lie because she had a plan all figured out. She didn't lie because she was blocking out the inevitable truth that awaited them. She said 'sure' because she knew that life always had a way of taking care of these things, whether you wanted it to or not. And life had this way of telling you when something was ending soon; prompting you to prepare. Much like red flags, the signs are always there, it's just that sometimes we choose to ignore them. But the girl was beginning to listen, embrace and accept that these types of situations would always fall under the Inevitable.

They leaned in and kissed sweetly, before she forced a smile and dragged her luggage across to platform 10. When she got on the train, it took all of her self-control to not look back. But when she sat down and realised she had succeeded in not doing so, she understood that she was going to be okay.

The DJ:

Hey Skye, sorry for being a bit absent recently.
The truth is I've met someone. I don't think I'm in love with her but I like her a lot.
She lives in Portugal but she's amazing!
I can't stop thinking about her.
She's a real woman, you know?
She's tough and responsible and just…amazing!
So here I am, sharing these things with you
Showing you my weaknesses
I always seem able to share things with you
I feel I can come to you with these things
The truth is you're probably one of only three people I feel I can confide in in London
I really thought you should know.
I care about you a lot.
And we have a lot in common.
I value that more than sex.
So please
I know this is asking a lot but
Can we be friends?

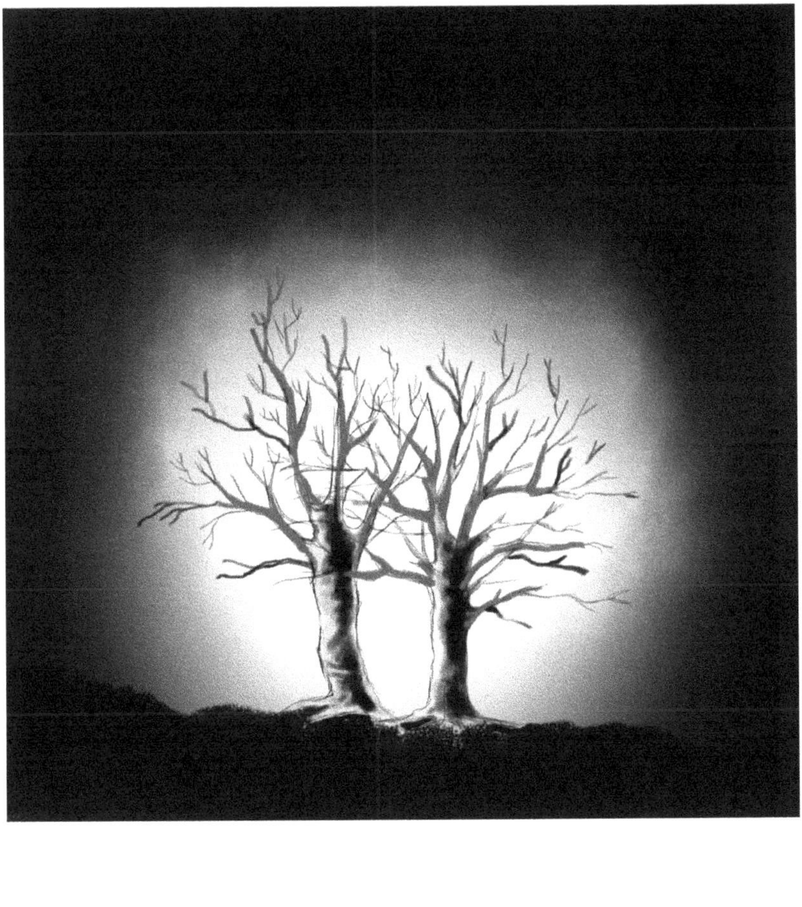

The girl cried and cried and cried into her pillow. At the humiliation, at the rejection, at the sheer nonchalant attitude the DJ had had when telling her about this girl he liked. They had not been together, she had not wanted something serious with him, hell, she had not even wanted to continue seeing him either, but...the feeling of rejection was unbearable. It flagged the awful words the Shark had once said to her. Words she couldn't even repeat to herself or bring herself to write about. They were too painful, too destroying.

    But spending time with the DJ had brought back some of her human side. To have that taken away, in a situation where she had had no say in the matter, was tearing her apart.

    She had built a wall so high up that not even she could see when she was being vulnerable to someone. And she had been vulnerable with the DJ, ever so slightly. And that ever so slightly was enough to hurt her pretty badly, considering her past experience. Rejection for the average person was bad, but with the girl, it was of epic proportions.

Yet she didn't know how to fix it, nor did she want to seem weak to the DJ.

And so she agreed to be his friend, even though he had hurt her. She saw no other choice. She couldn't seem to walk away without feeling weak or pathetic, and so she kept going back, kept showing him she was fine.

Because she was.
She was fine.

The Older You

When I entered the diner, I spotted Clara straight away, and we both squealed at the sight of one another, rushing in for a big hug.

"Skye! I haven't seen you in so long!" she shrieked at me, and we sat down at a table.

"I know! How are you? How are things?"

"Everything's good! What about you? Gosh, I haven't seen you in, what, two years?!"

Clara used to sit next to me at my old recruitment job. Remembering that office and remembering the Skye from two years ago, I felt like it was another person. I had just started seeing the Shark at the time, and had zero clue what I wanted to do with my life. How things could change in just 24 months.

*And it changed because **you** wanted to change it. This is all you, Skye.*

I inwardly smiled, as Clara told me about her new job.

"So you work there?" she asked me, pointing across the road at my beautiful work building, and I nodded. "Wow! That's great, Skye. Hey, how's the writing going? "Oh! By the way! I have a book for you..."

I frowned, as she dug her hand in her bag. "You got me a book?"

"I do! It's by a writer that reminds me so much of your writing, I think you should read it."

She handed me it and I stared at the cover in intrigue.

"Thank you Clara, this is very kind of you." I stared at the cover with some sort of feeling hitting me. It took me a while to realize that it was envy. I was envious of this person who had written a book, who had a book that they could hold in their hands. I felt in that moment just how much I wanted and craved the same thing.

"Oh please! So, tell me, are you writing any more pieces about the Shark?"

I looked up. "Why would I? That story is finished."

"Yeah but, it's the Shark – is it really ever finished?"

"Skye, learn to turn your weaknesses into strengths," the Shark used to say. "Your sensitivity is a strength. It makes you come back better and tougher than before."

Friends

The DJ and I sat on the steps of some abandoned government building on a suburban road in Kings Cross. How strange life could be. 8 million people in London and I had had to bump into the one person I had no intention of ever seeing again. Bumping into each other had led to a 'five-minute chat', and that five-minute chat had led to a 2 hour walk around Kings Cross, laughing and joking as if we hadn't ever been apart.

We now sat on those steps sharing a silence in the black of night. It was midnight, and the street was empty. The last person to pass us had been at least half an hour ago. The DJ was one of the few people in the world I was totally comfortable sharing a silence with. And I had forgotten how much I loved them.

"So I'm seeing this girl," the DJ suddenly said, snapping me out of my thoughts. "Second date tomorrow. Gonna take her to that Cuban place in Camden."

Oh wow, that didn't actually hurt. Maybe I can be his friend after all. Maybe I'm finally ready.

But I remembered how casually he had dropped me, told me he didn't want to kiss me or hug me or wake up next to me anymore; what he was essentially saying was that I was not good enough for him, and this hurt. This hurt like crazy. Even if I didn't want him that way, even if I had wanted to end it too. It was very painful for me to imagine he didn't think I was good enough.

And suddenly I could feel my chest tightening. It was nothing to do with him and I knew it, but he was only adding to my recently developed self esteem issues. And I realised then that I wasn't going to be able to be his friend.

I drifted off into thought as the DJ spoke about his dating life. I was again reminded that I had to let it go. It was fucking with my self-esteem. Maybe if I hadn't known the Shark I would have been okay, I would have laughed it off, I would have said to myself, *ha! These girls have nothing on me.* But I *had* met the Shark, he *had* fucked with my self-confidence, and I now needed to deal with these issues, whether I was ready to

or not.
"I'm still thinking about Camilla though," he told me. Camilla was the girl in Portugal he was crazy about.
"You should go over there if you really like her," I told him.
"You think so?"
"Yes." I said 'yes' but really my mind was elsewhere. My mind was already imagining my life without the DJ in it. I wondered how he would remember me.
That weird girl he had dated briefly.
I wondered if he would even remember anything about me other than our trip to Verona. In all honesty we had only seen each other a handful of times. I began counting all our meet ups as he continued to talk to me about Camilla.
It was an hour later that we stood at the westbound Piccadilly line platform of Caledonian Road tube station. The DJ turned to me with a nervous smile now, as my train approached, and I suddenly had a flashback of us standing at the platforms of Verona train station three months earlier. We had stood at those platforms having no real confirmation that we would ever kiss again, or stay up until 3am in his home studio talking about music or relationships. I hadn't had an impact on him, I was simply one of many, and I had to accept this without completely obliterating my self-esteem.
Promises of nothing have a way of coming to an abrupt end, and always before you're ready. Always before you've had time to mentally prepare.
It had hurt me much more than I had led the DJ to believe – his rejection I mean, and he had spent the last two months pushing for a friendship, a way of keeping me in his life.
I was attracted to him, but more than anything else I had somehow become emotionally attached to him. But I was not ready to accept this truth. To accept that after the Shark I was still able to get attached to people, to be human.
"I want you in my life, Skye. But I won't push, I can't. I think I've done everything I can. So if you can't find a way to be friends with me, then I will understand, and I will give up. But know that I am here, and if you feel you can, text me."

I gave him an appreciative smile and he pulled me into a tight hug, reminding me of the one we shared after our first date. Sadness consumed me, and as I held him close, I realised it was because I knew I would never text him. That this was it. That I was mentally capturing the moment to write about it later.

As we stood at the westbound Piccadilly line platform at Caledonian Road in a long, loving hug, I was appreciative of every inspiring thing he had ever said to me, of every time he had helped me, encouraged me, and listened to me. As I hugged him, I had a flashback of one specific night a couple of months back when he had just read some of my writing for the first time. I remembered his surprise at how good a writer he thought I was, of how he was so determined that I get published, and that I shouldn't let anything stop me.

I would take it all with me, his positivity I mean. And his wise words too, to form part of me, to remind me of his influence. But as I let go and ran onto the train, I realised I was not just sad, that a part of me felt good, too. A part of me felt healthier, as if I were starting to make good decisions again. It was a feeling I hadn't felt in a while. From before the Shark, in fact.

I needed to start looking after myself. And I knew then that this was the right decision, no matter how much it would hurt, no matter how much I would stare at his name on my phone, I was doing what was best for *me*. I would never be able to be his friend, and letting go of him was the right decision for both. I could neither be his friend, nor explain to him how many beatings to my self-esteem took place each time I looked at him.

What a trap it is - to be human but not have the courage to admit it.

But what a gift it is to understand that we carve our own path.

The DJ:

SKYE SKYE SKYE...SKYE
Now it's the business man talking, no bullshit
Regardless of the fact that I know you...
I am being very, very honest...
YOU ARE VERY TALENTED AT WRITING
Not just good...
VERY TALENTED
YOU NEED TO EXPLOIT THIS TALENT SKYE
I am serious...
You need to make writing the main activity of your life
No matter how difficult and long it will be getting there.
You have to do it.

Creativity is the essence of my being.

Back Here

Staring up at the ceiling in the darkness, I turned on my side to be met by the Shark's sleeping face. More than a year had passed, and yet here we were sharing a bed. Having not seen each other since the time I had turned up outside his office a few months back, and having broken up over a year ago, I wondered in what universe was it deemed normal for us to be sharing a bed.

The Shark hadn't laid a hand on me – we had reunited, broken the ice and then spent hours in amazing conversation, catching up on a year's worth of news. Missing my last train, he had then convinced me to stay until morning.

"Won't that be awkward for us?" I had asked.

"Come on Skye, it's me and you," the Shark had replied, and he had stayed faithful to his promise to keep his hands to himself. Even if when I had asked him to turn around so that I could change, he had laughed so hard anyone would have thought I had asked him to fly to the moon.

Watching him sleep, it took all of my self-control to not reach out and caress his face. The face that had channelled my inner shark. The face that had made me see that I could care for someone – the right person. That I could love unconditionally – the right person. The face in front of me had inspired piece after piece in the last year, writing that would now be going on to form my first book.

All my life I had believed that love was something you could switch on and off over time. Time gave you that power. And I had held onto that belief when I had agreed to see him. I had been looking for closure, you see. More than a year had passed and I was still writing about him – it did not seem normal. And so I had changed tactic. Rather than keeping him blocked on all technology, I had decided to confront my past and find peace.

But what I had yet to realise was that having power over love in any occasion was an impossibility. Love is something beyond our control, no matter how much time passes. It lives within us, taking its form and then becoming and remaining, indestructible. It is irreversible. Fighting it is futile; the only thing you can do is avoid its path. But I was not ready to accept this truth.

I am in control. I have stepped out of my feelings, I continued to repeat to herself, as I watched his peaceful face sleep.

He suddenly opened his eyes, and we stared at one another intensely in the darkness of his room. Not a word was uttered. We did not kiss, we did not move in towards one another. We simply remained in a powerful gaze. I had flashbacks of every moment we had ever shared together. The pain, the happiness, the closeness between us that was unique in every way possible. And I was overwhelmed with emotion.

But here's the thing. I didn't get up and shout 'this is a mistake!'

I didn't get changed and call a taxi.

Instead I remained completely still, looking back at him.

And as bizarre and illogical as it may seem, it was in that moment that I realised I held in my hands the closure I had been searching for all this time. But the problem had never been a lack of closure. The problem had always been my decision not to take it.

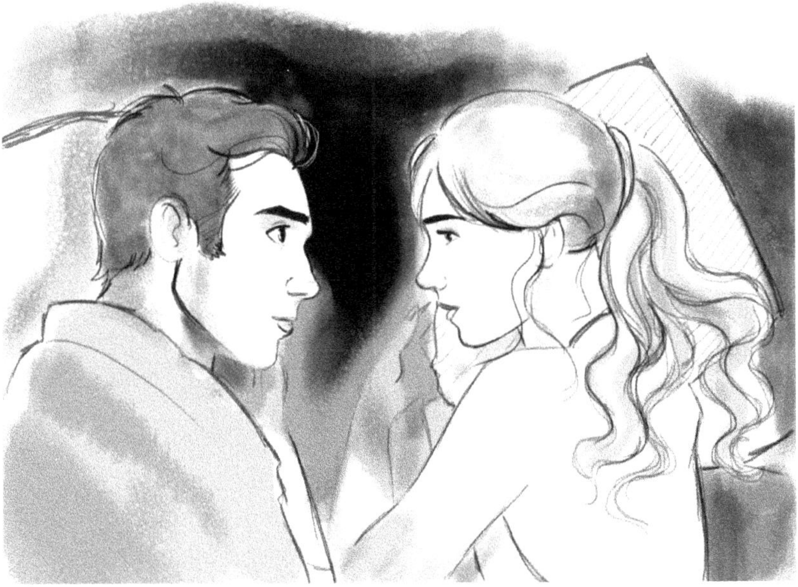

Hello Again

I walked anxiously down the dark streets of Notting hill, searching for his flat. The Shark had moved house since the last time we had seen each other. A group of loud 20-somethings passed me on the street, tipsy and ready for their Friday night out.

My phone suddenly buzzed in my pocket.

Shark:

Are you here?
Let me know if you're lost.

Skye:

The map keeps telling me I've arrived but I haven't.

Shark:

Send me a picture of where you are.

I did so, and waited for his response.

Shark:

Ok, go straight down, turn right, it's number 24.

I followed his instructions, walking down what seemed like a maze of flats. I turned around and read 'no 24' chalked onto the fence. I gulped as I put my phone away and pushed it open, knowing who would be standing on the other side of the gate. After all the months spent making sure to prevent this moment from happening – avoiding bars I knew he frequented, museums he liked, I had even avoided the entire Notting hill area in fear of bumping into him! And now here I was, walking into the lion's den, having unblocked him, and having been the one to suggest we meet.

He had messaged me three hours after I had unblocked him, and after an evening spent on the phone in which his stories had made me laugh until my stomach hurt, the next day he also helped me recover from a very bad presentation.

I was tired of thinking about him, of not being able to get over him, and I came to the conclusion that if blocking him wasn't working, I should try another tactic.

I would see him and talk to him and see if that brought me closure. It had to be worth a try.

I had suggested coffee, but he was sick with a fever and so I offered to make him my famous ginger and lemon drink. I didn't tell a soul I was going to see him, I mean, it was harmless, right? Who needed to know?

The gate creaked as I opened it, and I instantly spotted him standing next to door number 24, smoking a cigarette.

There he stood. After all this time.

"You found it!" he threw his cigarette to the ground and squashed it with the heel of his very expensive-looking black shoe. He was dressed in all black, in what looked like a brand new Dolce & Gabbana shirt, and his hair was different – still obscured in gel, but now they had brown highlights.

"Ciao, Skye."

I nervously approached, and the closer I got to his face the more I remembered just how much I loved every inch of it. I was instantly in love again, or maybe I had never stopped. All that time apart, and I was still crazy about him. He had broken me, ruined me, and I still loved him. It made me no fucking sense. I thought of that first night at that bar in Maida Vale. I had known then that I would fall in love with the bastard in front of me.

You had called him Bastard-eyes.

"Hi, stranger!"

He leaned in to give me the Italian tradition of pecks on

the cheeks, but I instead pulled him into a hug. The last thing I needed was his lips anywhere on my body. Taken aback, it took him a few seconds to react and hug me back. The hug was weak and lacked affection. Once we let go we smiled at one another, studying the other.

"It's been a while," he told me. "Come in, let me show you my new flat!"

"Okay."

I awkwardly stepped inside, cleaning my winter boots on the mat. "Do I need to...?"

"No, no, keep them on it's fine," he shivered, "it's so cold out there," he coughed, and my maternal instinct with him immediately kicked in.

"Are you okay?"

"Not really Skye, I've been off sick all week. It's a fever and sore throat that just won't go away."

I held out my grocery bag to him; it contained raw ginger and lemon. "Why don't I make this first and then you can give me a tour?"

"Great idea," we walked into the kitchen, but I found it bizarre for us to walk into a kitchen that wasn't his old one in his old flat, with no round glass table in sight. This kitchen was much smaller, and I felt instantly claustrophobic.

No Shark in so long, and now you're in such damn close proximity. What the hell are you doing, Skye?

But I thought of all the times I had researched his name on the Internet and checked his social media pages. I needed to find a way to get over him.

We awkwardly moved around the kitchen, bumping into each other. I didn't know anything about his new kitchen – where he kept his cutlery or his cups or anything. I was a complete stranger in his flat, and it gave me a sad feeling in my stomach.

I cut up the ginger and he watched me. "Are you going to observe me through the whole process?"

"Yes! This famous drink of yours, how many times you told me about it but I never had a chance to try it. I want to see if it works!"

I cut another piece and it flew across the kitchen top, hitting the tiles. I was so ridiculously nervous that I couldn't even cut ginger properly.

"Skye! Inventing a new sport? Some sort of flying ginger game? I feel it could catch on."

"Ha-*ha*, stop staring at me and do something – boil the water or something."

"Fine," he obeyed and I relaxed a little as I cut up the rest of the ginger. I sliced the lemon in half and by then the water had boiled, and the Shark's eyes were once again back on me, as he stood next to me. He was standing so close that the hairs on his arms were prickling against mine. The electricity running between us was intense. I had flashbacks of moments I had been so sure had been deleted from my memory. Small, irrelevant moments which were actually proving to be the most relevant.

Feelings came rushing back, along with a better view of the version of myself that I had been when I had met him – that feeling or belief that I could never be successful, so why even try?

I felt like it wasn't me, this person I was envisioning, but someone I had once read about or watched in a film.

"Okay you do it, I can't stand you staring like this anymore!"

He laughed and took the half slice of lemon from my hand, more electricity passing between us. Gently, he began squeezing into the cup of boiled water. "Like this?"

"Yep," I told him.

"And I wasn't staring at you, I was just wanting to see how you make it," he explained.

"You were staring like you always did whenever we cooked together."

"You were always scared of the boiling oil shooting out of the pan like a 5-year-old!"

"Er hello, it was boiling oil! It wasn't jelly babies!"

The Shark laughed, and suddenly squeezed lemon onto my bare arm. I shrieked dramatically, and he cackled as he repeated the act. I grabbed the other half of the lemon and squeezed it onto the back of his neck.

"No, Skye!"

I laughed and sprinted out of the kitchen, as he chased me. I flew through the living room just as he caught me, and I shrieked, in fits of laughter, as he squeezed lemon down my neck.

Suddenly the door slammed shut and we both turned to find a plump, Latin American man standing there with a rucksack.

"Hey Pablo," the Shark said to him, as he straightened himself out. I did the same, and smiled at the stranger.

"Evening," he said in a shy tone, walking passed us.

"Evening," I replied, and as soon as he had disappeared up the spiral staircase, I turned to the Shark for an explanation.

"Oh, he's my flat mate."

"What happened to Tommaso?!"

"He left me to go and live with his girlfriend."

I laughed to myself, and shook my head. "He probably thought we're on a date."

The Shark didn't change expression. "So what?"

"So what? We're not. We *used* to date, I am not one of your weekly conquests," I told him.

"Would you like me to go and tell him?"

"Hey-"

"I could just go and knock on his door, it's not a problem-" he made for the stairs, but I tugged at his arm.

"Don't you dare, Shark!"

"Why not? Don't think I could? I'm not Canned Tuna."

I smiled at him; hearing those words from that voice warmed my heart. It had been so long.

"Never have been, never will be."

We smiled at one another for a few seconds, before he threw his lemon in the bin. "Come on, let me give you a tour of the house."

It is impossible not to make mistakes in life. It is never impossible to learn from them.

"I have become a lot like you, you influenced me, I work all day-"

"Skye, do you think I'm happy?" the Shark asked the girl. She paused in her response, making a realisation she had not ever made before or connected with his success.

"No," she said, softly.

"I'm proud of you for finding your drive, I am. But do you think it's fun for me to focus only on work? To have no one around me? To keep everyone out?"

"But it's-"

"But it's what? Safer? You want to be more like me? Think twice. To everyone else your life will seem cool, but believe me, I pay for it every single day. I pay for what I did to you every single day."

Her Truth

I awoke at 3am, inches from the Shark's face. I began studying every part of it. It was incredible to think that more than a year had passed and I still loved him just as much as the day that I had left him.

And I had fallen asleep almost straight away – the Shark was the only person in the world that I had no problem falling asleep next to. My phone vibrated on the bedside table and I picked it up.

The DJ:

Hey Skye!!
How are you?
How's it going with the book?
I just had sex with that Brazilian girl by the way!
Finally! I feel so much better now.
Ready to go for my production session tomorrow!
Coffee next week? x

I sighed. I didn't understand it. In general the DJ was so good at reading people. Why couldn't he read that he had hurt me? That I was angry? He was a constant reminder of all my insecurities, and I hated having such insecure thoughts, this was not me. Usually I knew I was awesome. I guess after what had happened with the Shark I was slightly more susceptible to self-criticism than normal.

What am I doing? I need to get out of this. I need to let go of the DJ, he's not good for my self-esteem. I know he cares about me, I know, but I have to look after myself.

And why am I in the Shark's bedroom? How did I even end up here?

I put down my phone and glanced at the Shark's sleeping eyes. *He looks so harmless when he sleeps.*

209

He suddenly turned to lie on his back, and without opening his eyes, he gently pulled me towards him. As soon as my head hit his chest, it felt just as I remembered it:

Exactly like home.

I remembered wanting and wishing and hoping he would do this, all those nights we had slept in the same bed. I even remembered dreaming he was spooning me, only to be disappointed when I would wake up to find him all the way on his side of the bed.

I dug my face into his neck, taking in the scent that had always felt like it belonged to me too. He held me tightly, kissing my hair.

As magnificent as it felt, and as powerful as our connection was in that moment, I was instantly sad. Not because I knew this would probably be the last time I would ever be in such close proximity to the Shark, but because I knew there was a chance I would never love someone unconditionally ever again.

I've always found it mildly incomprehensible, how the kisses and hugs and attention from any one specific person could be so sacred to one human being, and so worthless to another.

Tu Sei Mia

Once I awoke the next day and remembered I was in the Shark's bedroom, I remained completely still. I tried to take in my choices, to understand my decisions, just as I felt the Shark shuffle around next to me. He was still spooning me.

"Buongiorno," he said.

"'giorno," I replied.

"Slept well?"

"Yes, you?" *Are we seriously going to small talk right now? Are we not going to acknowledge how fucking weird this is? To wake up next to one another? With you spooning me?!*

"Yes. The best I've slept in a long time."

How is it possible for two people that have not slept beside one another in so long, to do it so naturally and so organically, as if they had never stopped?

I couldn't wrap my head around it.

"Good. And your fever?"

"Much better." In the middle of the night, he had suddenly begun tossing and turning, and so I had quickly got up and got a cold towel to put on his forehead. Even in the middle of the night my maternal and loving instincts for him instantly kicked in. I found myself wondering if that would ever go away. If I were to bump into him on the street 40 years from then, I would probably be just as maternal with him as I was in that moment, and it was a very bizarre concept for me to accept. How love can truly last a lifetime.

"Good, I'm glad."

His hands began to move up and down my hips, and I wondered what the hell he was doing. It began to feel a little too familiar.

"Tu sei mia," he whispered in my ear, and I found myself smiling. All logic went out the window in an instant.

"I can't hear you, speak louder," I replied, feeling his warm breath reaching the back of my neck.

"Ah, still thinking you are more powerful than me? After two years? Really, Skye?" his hands continued to slide up and down my waist, seductively.

"And you still think you hold all the cards. Have you learnt nothing?"

"Sharp girl. What did I say on our first date two years ago, Skye? We are both able to read one another, but we both also like to win. It's imperative to both of us to win. The bad news is that someone always has to lose..."

"And it's not going to be me," I told him. I turned around and our lips instantly crashed into one another.

I was not able to resist his lips, his hands, his skin on mine. I had spent the last year craving it, imagining what it would be like to feel it just once more, to relive it just once more, to possess that connection just once more.

I knew we would not see each other again after this.

I knew it.

Life had a way of letting you know.

Life had a way of making you prepare.

And I had my luggage ready to go in the corner.

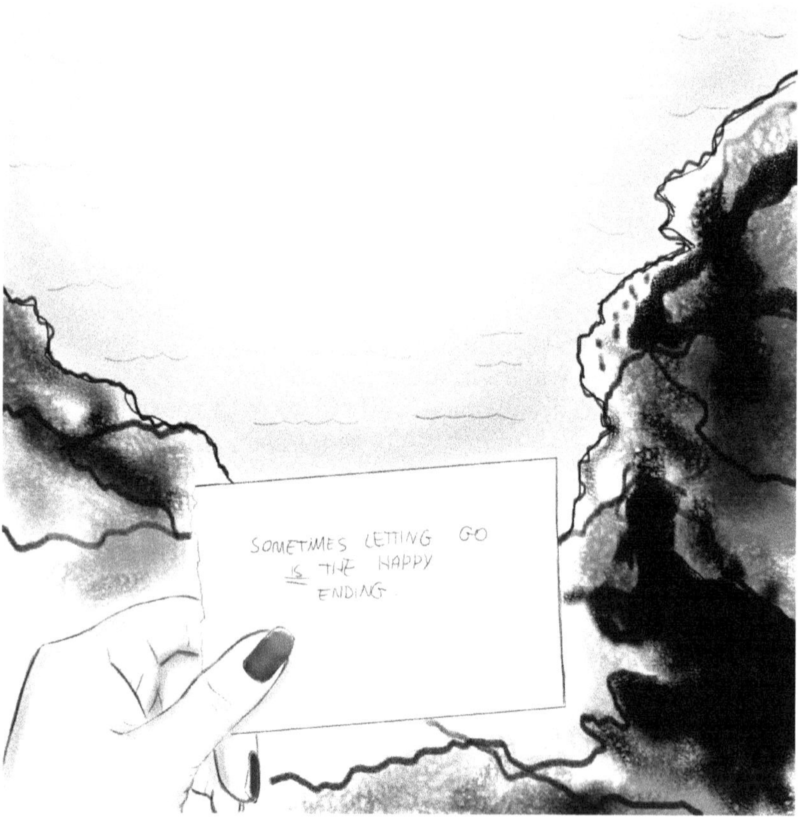
SOMETIMES LETTING GO
IS THE HAPPY
ENDING

The DJ:

Hi Skye
I've tried, I really have.
But I feel stupid messaging you all the time to check if you're still alive.
I won't be doing it anymore.
I wish you luck in everything you do, and that you get the best out of your many skills.
I still don't know the full story as to why you are this way, but I hope that one day you will drop your defenses to let other people get to know the real Skye.
Take care.

The Awards

With a third glass of white wine in hand, I immersed myself in the music, closing my eyes as I took in the moment, surrounded by my colleagues. Three months into my new job and it was no longer 'new'. I had worked hard, and loved every moment of it. I liked where I was, who I worked with, what I did, and the results I was starting to get.

This was the first time I was taking a break in a few weeks. I was working back-to-back, at my job, and on my book. I had deleted all dating apps from my phone – I had no time to date and no interest. I needed to focus on myself. I needed to see where I could go, what I was capable of.

I also wasn't talking to a lot of people, and since the DJ had stopped texting me I had realised just how much we had been in daily contact. To have it suddenly disappear left me with a certain void. Actually, if I'm honest it had left me with an overwhelming sense of sadness. But it was okay, I was going to be fine. I needed to let go, it was the right thing to do. I needed to do what was right for me.

My colleague Nicole clinked her wine glass with mine, and we smiled. We had said we would stay for one drink and then leave, but it was now 9pm and three glasses later. It felt good to relax, to forget everything and be a normal twenty-something, even just for one night.

"Everyone, quiet please! It's time for the awards," the director announced, and the music died down as all faces turned to look at the director on the small stage of the Shoreditch bar, and the massive, bright projector behind him.

"Oh I'm sure we're going to win," Nicole said to me, sarcastically.

"Oh yes, for sure!" I replied, just as sarcastically.

"Forget it, ladies – you can only start winning when you've been here at least a year," our colleague Nancy told us, clearly missing the sarcasm.

"This first one is for biggest influence on the company," the director began.

"Oh that's us for sure!" I squealed, taking a sip from my glass. My mind was still on the DJ, as I reeled from the news that I would no longer see his name pop up on my screen.

It's for the best, Skye.

"And the nominations are…Susanna…"

We cheered and clapped.

"Michael…"

More cheers and applause.

"James…."

By now I was bored with clapping and applauding, instead taking another sip from my glass and wondering if I could request the bar DJ to play 'Jump Around' by House of Pain.

"And Skye!"

I froze, as all heads turned to look at me.

"Woo! Well done!" Nicole shrieked.

Did he just say my name? I looked up at the stage to see my name on the screen, with my cheesy headshot next to it. *Oh shit, did I just get nominated?*

People continued to applaud and I blushed, wishing I had more white wine at my disposal.

"Shall I take a picture of that?" Nicole asked. "I'm taking a picture of that!" she took a photo of my name and headshot up on the screen.

"And the winner is…"

Am I about to win?

For biggest influence?

Am I really?

"James!"

My heart sank a little, and I clapped as James walked onto the stage to collect his award.

There was a strange feeling in my body. It wasn't just of disappointment, but of determination. In fact, I found that the determination was much stronger than the disappointment.

It's okay, I found myself telling myself. *This is just the beginning. There is so much still to do, Skye. So much.*

And you're going to do it all.

The hardest thing to do as an artist is constantly believe in your work before anyone else does.

The Moment

I didn't like the person I was turning into. I was too stressed, too tired to do anything. I was turning up to work dressed like a 12-year-old tomboy. I was crabby, could only watch films in 15 minute segments, and fell asleep at my laptop more than three times a week.

What for? All for a book? Did it seem right? A book that had no guarantee to be read by anyone other than my parents and brother. My brother would criticise every line of it for sure (out of love of course), and my mother would probably tell me how much she hadn't liked the Shark. Was it really worth all this effort?

It was one very warm night at the end of June that I sat in front of the laptop at 00:19am. I suddenly stopped the house music I had playing in the background, and stared at the screen,

In front of me was something I had created.

I had created a book! Something all mine. When had that happened?! *How* had that happened?! I could see seven-year-old me beaming next to me, telling me that Roald Dahl would be proud.

From start to finish, this thing was mine.

And it was ready.

I stared at the pages long and hard. These were pivotal moments in a writers' life. These were the moments that counted. These were the moments that made all the late nights and working weekends worth it. All the times I had locked myself away to write and edit, write and edit, write and edit...

This was the moment that counted the most. When you have a brief second to feel only pure and utter joy at what you have created.

My eyes dotted back and forth between my creation and my phone, my creation and my phone...

Until I was ready to ask myself:

Who do I want to share this moment with?

If you have to live by one rule, let it be this:

Let go of the people that are hurting you.

No matter how much you care about them.

No matter how much they care about you.

If they are hurting you:

Let. Them. Go.

Your future self will thank you. And remember, to heal a wound you must first acknowledge its existence.

My Choice

I stood at exit 4 of Old Street tube station looking everywhere for him, but as expected he was late. The air was warm and I was reminded that it was June in London.

Maybe this isn't a good idea, I thought.

Shut up Skye, you clearly want this. Stop being so stubborn and just give in.

If it goes wrong, if you feel you made the wrong decision, you can always bail, you can always tell him, you can always walk away. You are not committing to anything. It is simply dinner.

Where the hell is he?

It was 13 minutes later that I looked up to see him approaching. His warm eyes and smile made all my paranoia melt away.

"Hi," I said.

"Sorry I'm late, Skye!" the DJ leaned in, and gave me pecks on both cheeks. For a few brief seconds I remembered what usually happened when we were in such close proximity, but it quickly disappeared.

"I expect nothing less from you!" we began walking down the street together.

"Sorry, I was on a call and then left late!"

I felt myself tense up as soon as we started down the street, flashbacks pushing their way forward – Verona, his place...

How the hell is this going to work?!

"So where are we going?" I asked him.

"I thought we could go to this really nice restaurant in Shoreditch, or, we could go to my favourite Italian restaurant in Angel, it's really amazing...have you ever been to it? It's called La Gallina."

"No," I managed to reply.

"No way! How have we never been there together, it's my favourite restaurant..." his voice died away as he glanced at me. "Relax, Skye."

I gulped. "I *am* relaxed...."

"You're not, you're super tense."

Damn you for reading me. Can't you just read people on the street instead and give me the night off?

"I'm trying, it's just...this is weird."

"It doesn't have to be. We are simply two friends going to dinner together to catch up. A *long* catch up, since I haven't seen you in *months*! How's it going at work?"

"It's going alright, I booked my flight to New York..."

"Oh wow, you're really going!"

"I am indeed, for my birthday."

"Maybe I'll join you!"

"Don't you dare. This is *my* trip!"

"Well, aren't you nice."

"Oh!" I stopped in the middle of the pavement, and the DJ did the same, giving me a confused look as people rushed passed us. "I finished the book. It's out this summer."

The DJ beamed back at me. "Oh my God," he stared, stunned. "Oh my God... where is it? Do you have it? I wanna see it!"

"I haven't sent it to print yet."

"Well I want to see it! As soon as it's ready! Oh my God Skye, can you imagine holding in your hands your very own book? The first of many of course, but yours, all *yours!*"

I smiled as I watched him speak about my book with excitement. He was thrilled for me, and it was moving to see.

I had flashbacks of his motivating speeches when we had first met, and throughout the time we had been seeing each other. He had genuine interest in my work and my goals, just as I did with his.

Sure, he had had his inconsiderate moments, and there were probably more to come – no, actually, I was *sure* there were more to come. But let's not forget that I am not the easiest person in the world – he had definitely felt the wrath of my darker side on more than one occasion, and I have to say, he had been able to handle me impressively well.

"Skye, that's amazing! I can't believe it's finished. I can't believe..."

"Imagine no one likes it? Imagine it's hated?"

"It's normal for an artist to fear that. Just remember you're doing something incredible, Skye. Something incredible."

I smiled at him. "I wrote a book, Nicholas."

"You did indeed."

I pulled him into a hug, and he held me tightly. I closed my eyes as we hugged, people rushing passed us.

It was only then that my thoughts were confirmed: the DJ was the one I wanted to share this news with the most; he had always been there, listened and helped, given advice and genuinely cheered me on from the sidelines. We were both artists, and we understood each other not only when we struggled, but also when we triumphed.

The time we had not been talking I had felt something was missing. I'm not talking about sex, but the way he had always been a Friend. A friend I needed in this new version of myself. I cared about him immensely, and he had become a part of my life, I wasn't sure how, when or why, but it had happened, and I didn't want to lose him.

We began again down the street.

"Can't believe I've never taken you to my favourite restaurant."

"I think we spent most of our time at yours," I told him.

"Doing what?" he asked, playfully.

"Playing Scrabble, of course."

"Oh yes, now I remember!"

"So, how about you, Mr Funny Guy? How's it going with Camilla?"

I watched his eyes alight with love. "I think she might be the one. I might just be in love, I *might*."

"You *are*, you moron! You have been for months now."

"Fine, maybe you're right."

"So what are you going to do about it?"

"Well, I'm going out to visit her next week."

"Well done, proud of you. I know it wasn't the easiest step for you."

"Thanks," he suddenly pointed at something, "hey look,

that was where we had our first date!"

I glanced at the bar as we passed it, remembering us sitting inches from each other's faces as we shared stories. I had been so guarded, so antisocial, but in just a few hours with Nicholas I had brightened and relaxed.

"You had your game face on that night– *I'm gonna get her, I'm gonna get her.*"

"What does my 'game face' even look like?!" he asked me, curiously.

I creased up my forehead and narrowed my eyes at him, playfully.

"Beautiful! Thanks, Skye. I have the pulling face of a psycho."

I giggled.

"You're one to talk! You were so nervous that night you didn't even make eye contact the first half an hour of the evening!"

"I was so nervous to meet you!" I continued, "oh, did I tell you? I got nominated for an award at work!"

"What?! What for?"

"Biggest influence on the company!"

"Oh, look at you! A Shark under the surface, who would have guessed?" he put his arm around me, as we walked into the heart of Shoreditch with smiles on our faces. "Watch out everyone, this Shark is about ready to jump out.

Don't worry, as soon as your ego gets too inflated or you become a little too much like your ex, I'll be here to kick you back into place..."

"You are a modern day hero, aren't you?"

"I try, Skye. I really do."

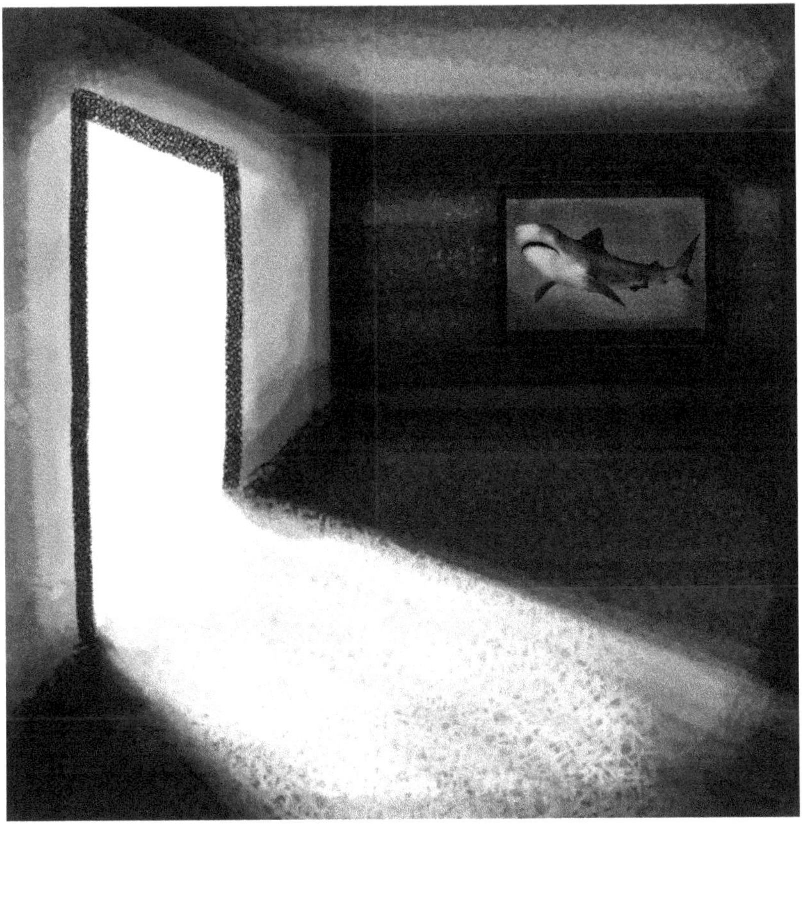

The Shark rushed over to the lifts at the same time as his colleague and friend, Charles. They nodded in acknowledgement to each other, as they got in and pressed '25'. The Shark smiled to himself in the silence of the lift.

"Good weekend I see," his colleague commented, snapping the Shark out of his daydream.

"Huh? Yes, it was. I met a girl – second date."

"You're always meeting girls," Charles replied with a smug look.

"Yes, but she's... weird. Interesting. She's a writer, even if I don't think she knows it yet. And she can make me laugh."

"Oh shit, what? I have to see that. The sex good?"

"Actually we haven't done it yet. We stayed up all night talking."

"PARDON ME? I think I just stepped into a teen chick flick. That explains your infatuation – you haven't nailed her yet. Don't worry, it will pass once you've banged her."

"You're probably right. But she's so funny, we were having dinner and she was telling a story when she stops to say, 'shit, are there foxes outside having sex?' and I thought it was part of the story and..." the Shark laughed to himself, whilst Charles just stared blankly at him. "I guess you just had to be there."

Bored with the conversation, Charles got out his phone to read a message. The Shark however, smiled to himself, and continued to do so all the way to the 25th floor.

Want to provide your feedback on Canned Tuna or share your story with Lisa Sa?

Email the author at the following address:

cannedtunabook@gmail.com

Or get in touch on the official Canned Tuna Facebook page:

www.facebook.com/CannedTunaBook

Lisa Sa is the Editor of online music publication the Stage Door, and blogs as Writer of Darkness on WordPress.

Born and raised in North West London, her writing is and continues to be inspired by the real life influences surrounding her, from local street gangs to the Britpop music scene. Lisa published her first book, Canned Tuna, in September 2017. It tells the story of twenty-something Londoner Skye, and what happens when she meets an arrogant and troubled man called 'the Shark'.

Lisa is driven by her two biggest passions: writing and music. She began the former at the age of seven, with short stories about talking animals. She went on to compose novels throughout her teenage years for the sheer purpose of developing her writing style. By the time she graduated from the University of Westminster, she knew her first definitive goal was to become a published writer.

Drawn in by the music industry at an early age, Lisa interned for Radio X during her gap year, and started her own radio show, Lisa's Takeover, on Smoke Radio. She went on to intern and/or work for several niche record labels and artist management companies, such as Sunlightsquare Records and ATC Management. She simultaneously wrote for online blog Musica, interviewing musicians and promoting new music. Lisa has met and worked with many honourable bands and artists.

WriterofDarknessBlog.WordPress.com
TheStageDoorOnline.com

Lightning Source UK Ltd.
Milton Keynes UK
UKHW021617080621
385145UK00009B/1674